BOWLEGS' BOUNTY

To Richard
Enjoy

Joseph Kropp

BOWLEGS' BOUNTY

Joseph Kropp

Day to Day Enterprises 🎆 *Oviedo, Florida*

Cover Design: Jamon Walker
Interior Book Design: Day to Day Enterprises

First American Edition

Printed in the United States of America
10 9 8 7 6 5 4 3 2 1

ISBN 13: 978-1-890905-24-8
ISBN 10: 1-890905-24-0

Library of Congress Cataloguing-in-Publication Data on file

This book is a work of fiction. And although Billy Bowlegs was a known pirate, I have fictionalized all accounts of his behavior and the company he kept. Any resemblance to actual events, locales or other persons, living or dead, is unintentional and coincidental.

Published by Day to Day Enterprises, Oviedo, FL
visit us at http://www.daytodayenterrprises.com

Acknowledgements

To my sons, whose enthusiasm for adventure inspired me to tell this story in the first place; to my wife Jerri, who suggested this book and many other fun endeavors over the years; to my father, whose campfire-side ghost stories scared me right into the warmth and safety of his lap; to my niece Kelly, my first reader and most honest critic; to my red-penciled crew – Charlie, Joy, Nannette, Susan, June, and Jerri (always Jerri); to my childhood friend who knows who he is and whose belief in me helped me believe.

Thank you all.

Joseph Kropp

Decisions

Family meeting. Everybody front and center."

Mr. Kaye was the kind of father who said things like "front and center," especially when he was about to discuss something exciting. The boys loved it when he talked like that. It meant he was in an adventurous mood, rather than the serious-minded way he usually had about him. Mrs. Kaye, on the other hand, did not love it when he said things like that because it generally caused the boys to come crashing down the stairs in a mad race to be the first to reach their father. Moms hardly ever liked crashing about in the house and this mom was no exception. What Mrs. Kaye did like, though, was a good adventure. She knew it sometimes took just that to get her husband to unwind and loosen up a bit. She understood it was hard for him to unwind. It was for her, too. The realities of keeping a family going with two active children and two working parents could be overwhelming. But, periodically, one or the other of them would get an idea for an adventure. It never took much persuading for everyone to get behind the plan, altering it, improving it, and embellishing it along the way.

This was one of those moments for the Kaye family.

"Boys, you don't need to run in the house. You'll break your necks bounding down the stairs like a pair of wild animals."

"Yes, ma'am," the boys yelled in unison, using their best manners. It would have been better if they had used their brakes instead, because they crashed into each other, hit the wall at the bottom of the landing, and ended up flat on their backs, side by side, at their father's feet. Mr. Kaye looked down to see two grinning boys lying at attention, giving their best regulation salutes.

"Um, at ease? Your mother and I have something to discuss with you."

"Yes, sir!" they both said, lowering their salutes.

"We have been talking, and talking often leads to discussion, and as you know, discussion can lead in many directions, one of them being conversation. And as we were conversing, it became apparent we were simultaneously arriving at a point of agreement, and, well, there you have it, your mother and I have agreed upon something."

"Gee, thanks for sharing, Dad." Benjamin was ten years old and self-appointed critic of his parents' character and behavior. He had sandy brown hair, a wise face, eyes that would one day cause female stomachs to do flips, and one heck of a jump shot. He tended toward the serious side, except when he was being silly.

Mr. Kaye was not to be dissuaded by his son's sarcasm, most especially not when that same son was still lying flat on his back in front of him. "There's more."

"Tell us, Dad. Hurry!" An eight year old with a mixture of Sunday school manners and 100% boyishness that was charm and imp rolled into one, Martin was a floppy red-haired, freckle-faced playmate or torturer to Benjamin, depending on which day it was, or which minute. He also played soccer and could usually be found with a ball in his hands, or juggling it in the air, bouncing it off his feet, or head, or the furniture, or one time, off one of Mrs. Kaye's favorite glass Christmas ornaments. After that, he mostly did his juggling outside.

"Well," Mr. Kaye continued, "as I was saying, after much discussion and conversation, not to mention talking..."

"Dad," groaned Benjamin.

"...after much of all that, we have agreed that it is high tide, uh, I mean time – high time we had an adventure of the nautical, oceanic, maritime, not to mention coastal variety."

"Huh?" said Martin.

"Don't ask," advised Benjamin. He knew what was coming, but it was too late to stop it.

"Mrs. Kaye, I see we have been remiss in giving these children a proper education about all things worldly and wet."

"I most certainly agree, Mr. Kaye. I believe a research expedition is in order. To the den, boys, and please walk in a civilized manner, not like a band of ill-mannered pirates."

"Benjamin, prepare the computer for take off. We will be visiting exotic locations on the World Wide Web."

"He means boot it up, right, Mom?"

"Precisely."

"Okay, what are we looking for?" asked Benjamin.

"The terms your father was using are all about the ocean, or the beach. We have decided to take a beach vacation."

"To the ocean!" cried Martin. "I've never been to an ocean before, have I?"

"Only once, when you were a baby," replied Mrs. Kaye.

"Yeah, you ran around in the sand with no pants on in front of everybody," offered Benjamin.

"I did not," Martin replied, giving Benjamin a hard look.

"You most certainly did, just the same as your brother did when he was a baby. I have pictures. I'm saving them for your wives."

"Aw, Mom," groaned Benjamin.
"That's gross," added Martin.
"Nevertheless," said Mrs. Kaye.

The Kaye family lived in the midwest. And one of the main parts of living in the midwest was the "mid" part. It was in the middle of the country, which meant that oceans, which tend to be on the edges of countries, were far away.

Benjamin brought up a map of the United States. "Looks like the Gulf of Mexico, by this skinny part of Florida, is the nearest ocean," he observed.

"That's not a real ocean," said Martin. "I learned the names of all the oceans in social studies this year. There's the Pacific, the Atlantic, and Indian, and I know there's one more, but it's not the Gulf of Mexico. That's only a gulf. It doesn't count as an ocean if it doesn't say 'ocean' in the name." Martin was quite pleased with himself for knowing, or mostly knowing, the names of oceans.

"The Gulf of Mexico counts," Mrs. Kaye assured him. "It's part of one of the oceans."

"Yes," added Mr. Kaye. "And maybe you boys could figure out which one, and while you're at it, you can come up with the name of that other ocean you forgot, Martin."

"That skinny part of Florida is called the 'panhandle,'" said Mr. Kaye.

"Okay, so is that where we should focus our search?" asked Mrs. Kaye.

"Yes," said the boys.

As they narrowed their search and began exploring locations along this stretch of Florida, they began to learn some details. After a few keys strokes, Benjamin said, "It looks to be about 1,000 miles from here."

"How long is that in the car?" Martin wanted to know.

"We can average about 50 miles an hour, so how many hours would that be, Benjamin?" asked Mr. Kaye.

"That's 20 hours," reported Benjamin. He was quick with numbers.

"So if we drive 12 hours on the first day..." began Mrs. Kaye.

"We'll have eight hours left the second day," finished Martin after a quick count on his fingers. He did not want Benjamin to show him up in the math department.

"We could be on the beach by mid-afternoon of the second day if we get up and leave early," Mr. Kaye observed.

Benjamin had narrowed his search to a part of the Florida panhandle that sounded particularly inviting.

"Mom, Dad, look at this."

They crowded around the computer, Martin squeezing his head through.

"I get to look, too."

"Of course you do," said his mother. "What have you found, Benjamin?"

"A part of the panhandle called the Emerald Coast."

"The Emerald Coast," repeated Mrs. Kaye. "Doesn't that sound interesting?"

"Is the coast made of emerald?" asked Martin. He was already thinking about how many would fit in his suitcase.

"No stupid, not real emeralds."

"Hey."

"Benjamin?"

"Sorry, Mom, sorry Martin."

"That's better. So why do they call it the Emerald Coast?" asked Mrs. Kaye.

"It says here," said Mr. Kaye, reading from the screen, "because of the emerald green waters of the gulf, set off strikingly by the brilliant white sandy beaches."

"Oh, it sounds lovely,' said Mrs. Kaye.

"It does indeed. What do you boys think?"

"When can we go?" wondered Martin.

"Your mother and I have cleared our schedules three weeks from now. We will be able to leave on a Saturday, arrive on Sunday, and have six nights there before we come home."

"Alright," said Martin. "Can I go tell my friends?"

"Certainly," said Mrs. Kaye to Martin's back. He wasted no time in heading for the door.

"I think I'll call some of my friends," said Benjamin.

After the boys left, Mr. and Mrs. Kaye continued searching for information on the computer. They intended to have a few surprises prepared to make the trip all the more memorable.

♐

The boys didn't know how they could wait for three weeks to pass. But, with all the planning and preparation, the time really did go by quickly. Mr. and Mrs. Kaye had reserved a beachfront condominium, complete with a kitchen and two bedrooms. The unit even had two beds for the boys. Martin was a kicker and Benjamin always stole the covers, so sharing a bed was never fun for them.

Mrs. Kaye made a list of things to pack for a week at the beach. Her list included things like underwear, socks, towels, and the like. The boys made their own list of more important stuff like snorkels, fins, masks, pails and shovels, just in case they really did find emeralds on the beach. Mr. Kaye was in charge of preparing the family van by getting an oil change and checking air in the tires. The boys helped him wash the car inside and out.

When the night before their trip finally arrived, the boys set their alarm clock to prepare for an early departure. It was like going to bed on Christmas Eve. They talked about the fun they would have until they couldn't stay awake any longer. Finally, the boys slipped into dreams of snow-white sand, blue-green waters, and beautiful deep green emeralds.

The Journey

Jt was a long day in the car. The odometer showed they had traveled well over half way when they pulled into the motel for the night. Although weary, they all felt a sense of accomplishment. There was also an excitement that had begun to grow with every mile as their destination got closer and closer. They had worked together to make their car journey as pleasant as possible. The boys only bickered when they felt it was absolutely necessary. And after about the tenth time of asking, "Are we there yet?" and getting the same answer from their father – "Yes we are, we've been there for three weeks now. It's all a state of mind" – they found other ways to occupy themselves. They read books, played hand-held video games, and Road Sign ABC's, often arguing more than playing. But somehow, it all worked to make the time go faster. Just when they were about to go crazy from being in the car so long, Mrs. Kaye produced brochures she had ordered from the Chamber of Commerce.

"Thanks, Mom," said the boys as they began to study them. The pictures of parasailing in the Gulf of Mexico intrigued Benjamin.

"Whoa, look at this. I'll bet you could see everything from up there," he said, showing the picture to Martin and to Mrs. Kaye. "Do you think we could try this?" he asked.

"I think that's a fine idea. I just hope we don't run into any pirates out on the high seas."

"Mom, there aren't pirates anymore," said Martin.

"Well, you never know, boys. It's an awfully big ocean. No telling what might be out there."

"It says here," said Benjamin, "in the 1800's, a pirate named Billy Bowlegs buried treasure all over the Choctawhatchee Bay."

"I thought we were going to the Gulf of Mexico, not the Choctawachamacallit Bay," said Martin.

"The Choctawhatchee Bay connects to the part of the Gulf of Mexico we're visiting," explained Mrs. Kaye.

"Cool. Maybe we can dig for buried treasure," said Martin. "We brought our shovels."

"Those stupid plastic shovels aren't going to be much help digging for treasure," said Benjamin.

"How do you know? You've never dug for pirate treasure," Martin argued.

"No, and I'm not about to. You think you're the only one who's ever thought about finding treasure? It's probably all been dug up years ago. You'll look pretty stupid digging holes all over the place, thinking you're going to find something."

"Well if I do find something, I'm not sharing it with you."

"Fine."

"Fine," added Martin, closing the discussion.

Mr. Kaye told Martin he could dig all he wanted. "Who knows?" he said. "Stranger things have happened. With the tides and the winds changing the lay of the land like they do, you might just come across something that's been hidden for hundreds of years."

"Yeah, I bet I will," said Martin.

8

"You might also make a discovery on the ocean floor. Lots of treasure was lost at sea, too."

"Oh yeah," said Martin, "this is going to be great!"

"I've heard those who find pirate treasure sometimes get more than they bargain for," said Mrs. Kaye.

"What do you mean?" asked Benjamin.

"I'm sure it's nothing. It's just I've heard some people believe the pirate's ghost guards his hidden treasures."

"How do they guard the treasure?" asked Martin.

"I've read about different ways," said Mrs. Kaye. "Sometimes they follow the person who finds it, or I should say people who have found pirate treasure have *felt* like they were being followed by a ghost."

"Well, how long do they feel that way?" asked Benjamin.

"Until they get rid of the treasure – or return it," said Mrs. Kaye.

"Are you making this up, Mom?" asked Martin.

"I can't say if the stories are true. Probably they're just part of the fun of thinking and talking about pirate treasure."

"Doesn't sound like much fun to me," allowed Benjamin.

"Me neither," said Martin.

Those conversations, and others, helped the time go faster. Toward the end of the drive, Benjamin asked if his father knew how to get to the motel they had chosen for the night.

"What do you mean, Benjamin?"

"Well, we've been driving forever. I thought maybe you missed a turn or something."

"Dad knows what he's doing, Benjamin. Don't you Dad?"

"Yes, Martin, I do. Your mother and I carefully mapped out our course and have followed it to a tee," boasted Mr. Kaye. "Isn't that right, dear?"

"Except for the time I told you to go east and you thought we were supposed to turn west."

"But we corrected our course straight away, didn't we?"

"After you took that short cut," said Mrs. Kaye.

"And even though that didn't exactly work out, we did find our way back to right road."

"And I don't think your short cut took us more than 10 or 15 miles out of our way."

Martin groaned. "Are you sure we're going the right way now?"

"Absolutely," said Mr. Kaye.

"No offense, Dad, but are we, Mom?" asked Benjamin.

"I'm keeping a close eye."

"Good," said both boys in unison.

When they finally arrived at the motel for the night, the Kaye family was happy to pile out of the car and get to their room. Within a few minutes, the boys brushed their teeth, washed their faces, and changed into their pajamas, which consisted of just pajama pants these days. Not long before, Benjamin had joined a few of his friends at a spend-the-night party and noticed all the boys his age slept in just pajama bottoms. It wasn't long after Benjamin had taken up the habit, that Martin decided it wasn't cool to wear a shirt to bed. The boys negotiated which side of the bed each would have, and Martin warned Benjamin not to steal the covers.

"What are you going to do, kick me? You'll do that all night anyway."

"Be quiet, Benjamin Franklin."

"Sure thing Marty Farty."

"Boys!"

"Sorry, Dad," said Benjamin

"Me too," added Martin.

After all that, they finally settled their heads onto their pillows. Mr. and Mrs. Kaye sat on the edge of the other bed and waited for the inevitable request. It came from Martin.

"Dad, will you read us a bedtime story?"

"No, Martin, but I will tell you one."

"Great," said Martin.

"Alright," added Benjamin. "I'm not really sleepy anyway."

"How nice," said Mrs. Kaye as she climbed into bed to listen too.

Mr. Kaye got a far off look in his eyes, as if he was remembering something from a long time ago. His voice took on a different kind of tone. Martin, Benjamin, and Mrs. Kaye wondered what was coming next.

The Long and Fateful Journey

A long time ago, life on the high seas was wild and fearsome. And the most wild and fearsome man on the high seas was none other than the pirate, William Augustus Bowles, better known as 'Billy Bowlegs.'

"Alright, a pirate story!" said Martin.

"Be quiet," barked Benjamin.

"You be quiet," responded Martin.

"Boys," cautioned Mrs. Kaye.

"Sorry, Mom."

"Me too," added Martin. "Make it a scary story, Dad," said Martin.

"Yeah, real scary, Dad," said Benjamin.

"Yeah, but not too scary," said Martin.

"It'll be alright, I'm sure," said Mrs. Kaye.

All who traveled the high seas feared Billy Bowlegs. Trading vessel captains who knew his reputation avoided him at all costs, sometimes risking dangerous routes just to keep away from him and his band of sea dogs. More than one ship was scuttled on the rocks as they sailed too close to islands, trying to hide from the watchful spyglass of Captain Bowlegs.

His ship carried more cannons than most military vessels. Unarmed trading ships were easy targets for Billy and his band of buccaneers. Even other pirates gave him a wide berth if they were sailing in the same waters.

The name Billy Bowlegs was known far and wide. Nobody was really sure who he was or from where he hailed. Some said he was a discontented bookkeeper who had been employed by a rich factory owner. The story was told that one day, Mr. Bowles simply disappeared, along with a sizeable portion of his employer's fortune. Others guessed he was a British Navel Officer whose ship had been captured by pirates and, after joining them, the ruthless Mr. Bowles eventually led a mutiny and took the ship for his own. His habit of wearing the frock of a British officer gave credence to those who believed in the naval origins of Captain Bowlegs. His true identity remained a mystery until the day he died. But, whoever he was and wherever he came from, his name became the most feared and dreaded of all the pirates who harvested their bountiful riches on the high seas.

This story is about the first time Billy Bowlegs sailed his ship, the *Tell No Tales,* to the Emerald Coast. He and his crew had been sailing for days and days, and it seemed as if they had traveled a thousand miles. Billy was in his cabin when there was a knock at the door.

"Come in then, if ya must disturb me thoughts," was the reply the first mate got for his troubles. His name was John Smelling, but he was known as 'Smelly John,' and not just because of his name. He was also the biggest man Billy had ever seen or wanted to see. He looked like – well, I guess he looked like a pirate. He had a large gold earring in one ear, thick, heavy whiskers, and long, greasy hair that hung over his shoulders, which he covered with a blood-red do-rag.

☠

"A do-rag, Dad? I doubt they had do-rags in pirate days," challenged Benjamin.

"Well, that's what it looked like, even if they didn't call it that."

"I have to go to the bathroom," said Martin. "Will you wait for me?"

"Of course," said his mother.

Of course, when Martin emerged from the bathroom, he had fashioned his own version of a do-rag out of a hand towel.

"Now you look just like a pirate," observed Mrs. Kaye.

"Smells like one, too," said Benjamin.

"Do not," yelled Martin as he pounced on Benjamin, tussling with him until both boys fell off the bed, pulling most of the covers and pillows with them.

"So that's the way things are, are they? I guess we'll just have to take you two young marauders prisoner. Mrs. Kaye, do you remember what we did with those last two sea dogs we caught committing heinous acts of bed-disheveling and roughhousing?"

"Oh, I'm not sure I do," said Mrs. Kaye. She was going along with the game. She just wasn't quite sure where the game was going.

"Why, we made 'em walk the plank," said Mr. Kaye with his best attempt at sounding pirate-ish.

"Of course. They walked the plank. How could I forget?"

☠

As the boys wondered what their father was up to, their mother, who was usually full of surprises of her own on a trip, went to her suitcase and pulled out a beautiful plastic replica of a pirate saber. It had a rhinestone-jeweled handle and even had a decorated scabbard.

"I believe you'll be wanting this, Captain Kaye," she said, handing him the sword ceremoniously. (Of course, there were two swords in her bag, meant to be brought out and given to the boys at just the right time.)

Martin and Benjamin stood by the bed, wondering what was happening. Whatever it was, they thought it was fun. And no one had made them make up the bed so far, which was a good thing as far as they were concerned.

"Thank you. Now men, we'll not be having all manner of rowdiness and roughhousing as were displayed here tonight. Not in my crew we won't. The penalty on the high seas for such behavior is a long walk off a short plank. Mrs. Kaye, would you kindly slide that door open so I can escort these two roughs to their doom?"

"Certainly."

"Alright men – march." Mr. Kaye marched them at sword point out the door and around a hedge. When the boys saw the pool and diving board, they realized their father wasn't joking.

"If you haven't noticed, Dad, we're in our P.J.s," Benjamin pointed out.

"Shouldn't we change into our bathing suits?" asked Martin.

"I don't expect Davey Jones has much of a dress code. He just wants your bones, I'll wager. Now up on that plank, the both of you."

As they stepped up onto the board, Martin wanted to know who Davey Jones was.

"It's an expression," Mrs. Kaye explained. "Pirates referred to the bottom of the sea as 'Davey Jones' Locker.' Sorry to interrupt, but their education is so important."

"I quite agree. No problem at all."

"Yeah, too bad we won't be around to study up on Davey Jones, seeing as how we'll just be bones at the bottom of the ocean," said Benjamin. "Goodbye cruel world," he added. Then, placing the back of one hand on his forehead and the other over his heart, he said, "Alas, I am too young to die," took a final step off the board, and plunged into the inviting water below.

"Alice, whoever you are," said Martin, "I'm too young to die, too." And with that, cannonballed into the pool, doing his best to splash his parents. He just missed.

The boys played in the pool, reenacting their drops to a watery grave. When it was time to get out of the pool and ready for bed again, each parent wrapped a boy in a towel and helped to dry them off. While Mr. Kaye found a pair of dry pajamas for the boys, Mrs. Kaye wrung out the wet clothes and hung them to dry in the bathtub. As he was toweling off his wet hair, Martin asked, "Are you going to continue the story now, Dad?"

After the late night swim, the boys were as wide-awake as ever. "I suppose I'd better. Then we can all get some sleep."

Benjamin flopped back down on the bed (which had been quickly remade by Mr. and Mrs. Kaye while the boys were getting ready), put his hands behind his head, and said, "Ready when you are, Dad."

"Me too," said Martin, resting his head on his hands, too.

"Ok, where was I?" Mr. Kaye thought out loud.

"Smelly John had just interrupted Billy Bowleg's thoughts," said Martin.

"That's right, Martin. Well, then, Billy said…"

"What is it you'll be wantin from me, John?"

"Well, sir, we have a situation with the men, sir. Couple

of'em is sayin they been out at sea too long, and well, sir, they think we're never goin to hit land at this rate, and, well, beggin yer pardon, sir, some even wonders if you know where yer headed."

"That's what they're sayin is it? Well I expect by tomorrow they'll know different."

"Yes, sir, Cap'n, sir, only some'a the other men is listenin and startin to have doubts too. I'm afeard someone is gonna get so worried, they'll try somethin desperate, sir."

"Are they talkin mutiny, then?" wondered Billy, his irritation growing.

"No. No, sir not yet. It's just I'm afeared it'll come to that if you take my meanin. I think they need ya to set'em straight, sir."

"If I have to set'em straight, I believe I'll set'em off – off the plank." With that, Billy got out of his chair and put on his coat. Smelly John hurried to open the cabin door and stood aside as Billy swept out of the cabin and up onto the deck. As he approached his crew, he noticed they looked guilty, as if they had just been talking about him and probably saying some rather unkind things.

"I hear there's some as is wonderin if I know what I'm doin, wonderin if I can find me way to the Emerald Coast. I expect I can find me way in any water ya care to put me in. But if any of ya is displeased with my captain'en, well yer welcome to draw yer wages and put off when we get to shore, which will be tomorrow by my reckonin. Those that's want'n to leave now, well I hope ya can swim. And any that thinks they know more than I do about sailin this ship, or has notions about takin over, well, I'll be happy to introduce ya to the tip of me sword and escort ya to the end of the plank. Anyone yearnin fer a change in situation, just step right up and be dealt with."

None of the pirates moved nor said a thing. None would even make eye contact with the captain. It seems pirates are like other types of bullies. Their bark is often worse than their bite. No one wanted to challenge Billy when it came right down to it.

When no one stepped up, Billy said, "Fair enough then. Tomorrow we sail into harbor on the Emerald Coast, the richest and most bountiful of all seashores. It's fun we'll be havin helpin ourselves to the loot of every ship that dares enter the harbor while we're there. Tomorrow, the Emerald Coast!"

"The Emerald Coast!" shouted the crew.

"And that is where we will leave Billy and his band of pirates for tonight," said Mr. Kaye.

"Good story, Dad," said Benjamin.

"Yeah," added Martin.

The lights were turned out as everyone settled in for a rather short night of rest.

"Pirates certainly use poor grammar, don't they boys?"

"Mom that's how pirates talk, they don't have to worry about teachers or mothers telling them to talk different."

"Different*ly*, Benjamin."

"Oh, right," said Benjamin.

"We're getting to the Emerald Coast tomorrow and so is Billy Bowlegs," said Martin. "I wonder if we'll run in to him."

"We might just do that," said Mrs. Kaye, giving her husband a knowing smile.

"I suppose we might," Mr. Kaye responded.

The boys weren't sure what to make of that, but they were too tired to worry about it. As he was about to fall asleep, Martin remembered something he had meant to ask.

"Hey, Benjamin, who's Alice?"

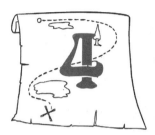

The Emerald Coast

Because they had traveled so far the previous day, the Kayes looked forward to arriving by early afternoon. And though it was a short night, it was no trouble waking everyone and getting moving in the morning. Mrs. Kaye was the first up and the boys quickly followed. She wished they would jump out of bed with as much enthusiasm on school days. Mr. Kaye was the last one out of bed, but it never took him long, once he was up, to get ready for the day. In no time at all, everyone was dressed (the boys in their swimsuits so as not to waste any time once they got to the beach), packed, and loaded into the van. As they pulled out of the motel parking lot, Mrs. Kaye, always full of surprises, produced an entire picnic breakfast out of one of her bags. By the time they were back on the highway, the boys and their father were treated to orange juice, fruit flavored yogurt, string cheese, and donuts.

"Great van picnic, Mom," said Benjamin.

"Can I have another donut?" asked Martin.

"You can have mine, Martin. You know how I like to watch my waistline," offered Mr. Kaye.

"Do you happen to know why two donuts were missing from the box this morning?" asked Mrs. Kaye.

"Oh, well, starting now, I'm on a diet. Got to look good in my bathing suit, you know."

"Right," said Mrs. Kaye.

Later that day, they stopped for a quick lunch and then got right back on the road. Not long after that, they turned onto the road that paralleled the beach, and would take them to the condo they had rented for the week. They were right on schedule to arrive at the earliest possible check-in time. The Choctawatchee Bay, a part of the Intracoastal Waterway, was on one side of the road and the Gulf of Mexico on the other. Finally being near the water was exciting and Martin immediately began keeping a lookout for Billy Bowlegs' ship.

"He could be out there." said Martin. "He was due to arrive today."

"Yeah, about 200 years ago from today," pointed out Benjamin.

"You never know," said Mrs. Kaye. "We may see Captain Bowlegs before the day is through."

"I wouldn't be surprised if you're right," said Mr. Kaye, going along with the joke.

"Yeah, right," said Benjamin

"I hope we do," said Martin. "I'd give Billy Bowlegs a taste of my sword."

Mrs. Kaye had given the boys their swords as soon as they crossed the Florida state line. They avoided doing any damage with them – especially to either parent. That would be a crime punishable by being disarmed. Now, Martin brandished his sword like a buccaneer of old.

"Yes, sir, if Captain Bowlegs gets near me, he'll know what hit him. I'll sword fight him."

"You'd run like crazy if you ever did see a pirate," guessed Benjamin.

"Would not," Martin asserted. "I'd run him through with my saber. Billy better watch out for me if he knows what's good for him."

"Whatever," sighed Benjamin.

"Would you look at that water," said Mr. Kaye.

"And that awesome beach," said Benjamin. "I can't wait to dive into the water."

"I bet I reach the water before you do," challenged Martin.

"We'll see about that," responded Benjamin.

"The water looks so beautiful. I can certainly see why they call this the Emerald Coast. And that sand, if I didn't know better, I'd say we'd arrived just after a snow storm. I've never seen sand so white," said Mrs. Kaye.

"Neither have I," said Mr. Kaye. It definitely lives up to it's reputation as one of the most beautiful beaches in Florida."

"Or anywhere else in the world," said Martin. "This is the best beach ever!"

As they drove along, they saw jet skis for rent, miniature golf courses, go cart tracks, and water slides. Someone was parasailing high out over the water. At one intersection, they drove by a tall, metal platform just in time to see a bungee jumper plummeting down and then springing up again as he reached the end of his tether. Benjamin thought he resembled a human yo-yo. They soon passed an arena that boasted a show of dolphins and other sea creatures. The boys quickly worked on getting a commitment from their parents to make a trip back for that. Minutes later, they turned into the Gulf View Condominiums, their home away from home for the next week. Martin spotted the pool.

"No diving board. I guess we won't be walking the plank at this pool," said Martin.

As Mr. Kaye parked the van and headed for the office, the boys were shedding shirts and shoes.

"Can we go to the beach, Mom?" asked Benjamin.

"Just for a few minutes while we're checking in. After that, we'll need you boys to help unpack the van and get us all moved in," said Mrs. Kaye. "And don't go out in the deep water until we can watch you."

"I'll beat you," shouted Martin, getting a head start while Benjamin negotiated with Mrs. Kaye.

Benjamin was not about to let his younger brother bet him. Martin gave it all he had, but just before reaching the water, Benjamin passed him, yelling, "Last one in is Smelly John."

The water felt perfect. Not too cold, just cold enough to be instantly refreshing on a hot day spent cooped up in the car. Their first taste of the sea water was a surprise. They knew, of course, the ocean was salt water. They just hadn't thought it through enough to consider it would *taste* so salty. After splashing around in the water awhile, they figured it was time to help unload the van and get moved in. Just then, they heard their mother calling. She waved from a balcony three floors up. Their unit was on the corner of the complex, allowing front and side views of the beach.

"Hello, boys. Wait until you see the view from up here. It's specatcular. I can see for miles down the beach."

"What's the room like, Mom?"

"Wonderful, Benjamin. There are two beds in your room, just like we wanted. There's a nice big kitchen and this balcony comes off a large family room and there's even a side entrance from the master bedroom. Your father just went back down to the car. Help him bring a load up and come see for yourselves."

"Sure, Mom. We'll be right up," said Benjamin.

They found their father and helped him unload their stuff. Getting on the elevator, Mr. Kaye said, "push three."

"We know, we saw Mom out on the balcony," said Martin.

The boys loved the condo. The master bedroom, kitchen, and family room were just as Mrs. Kaye had described.

Their bedroom was large with plenty of closet space. They even had a sliding glass door leading to a small balcony overlooking the pool. There was another amenity the boys were happy to see.

"I get the bed by the T.V," said Martin.

"Oh no you don't," countered Benjamin. "I'm older, I should get the first pick and it just so happens I like that bed right there," said Benjamin, pointing to the bed nearer the T.V.

"You don't get to choose just cause you're older. I called it and I'm keeping it." Martin sat on the bed, suitcase in hand, and stared defiantly at his brother.

"Get out of my way, pipsqueak," demanded Benjamin.

"No way. This is my bed," argued Martin.

"I said get off," said Benjamin.

"Make me, stupid."

"I don't have to. You already are."

Martin stood up and Benjamin stepped toward him. They would have engaged in battle except for the timely intervention of their parents, who had come to the open door of their room to investigate the raised voices.

"What's going on here?" asked Mr. Kaye.

Both boys started talking at once, pleading their respective cases. It didn't work.

"Benjamin, you know we do not tolerate bullying just because you're older and bigger," said Mrs. Kaye.

"I can handle him," said Martin.

"That's not the point," said Mr. Kaye.

"In your dreams, maybe," responded Benjamin.

"That's enough. We didn't drive all this way to fight over a television set."

"Your father is right, boys. I'm sure we're all a little tired from our long journey. But you have to learn to handle conflicts like civilized human beings. We don't come to blows over a discussion about who gets which bed."

"But I called it," pleaded Martin. "If I called it, I should get it."

"I agree, Martin. Because you called it first, and because we'll not tolerate bullying in our family, you shall have the bed by the T.V."

"Great, Martin gets his way, as usual," said Benjamin.

"And that will continue as long as you try to throw your weight around with him," Mr. Kaye pointed out. "Do you understand, Benjamin?"

"Yes, sir,"

"Thank you for doing the right thing, Mom and Dad," said Martin.

"I wouldn't press my luck if I were you, Martin," said Mr. Kaye.

Benjamin glared at his brother. His demeanor brightened, however, as Mrs. Kaye told Martin the unhappy news. It didn't matter who was closer to the T.V. because there would be no T.V. watching on this trip anyway.

"Why?" wondered Martin.

"Because we have just arrived at the beach, a location we chose several weeks ago. And after planning this trip, driving for the better part of two days, and finally arriving in this stunningly beautiful location, there is absolutely no reason on earth why you should spend your time sitting in front of a television set watching shows you could have stayed home to watch."

The boys knew when Mrs. Kaye got rolling with a lecture, their best strategy was to stop arguing. They weren't going to win anyway and more arguing would just lead to more lecturing. She had a lot of stamina when it came to lecturing.

During the argument, they had forgotten for a moment they were in a hurry to finish unloading the van and get back outside where the action was. From their room, they could hear sounds of splashing and kids playing in the pool. They went out on their balcony to look.

"Nice pool, huh?" said Benjamin.

"Yeah," said Martin. "I guess it doesn't matter which bed I have. Take either one you want."

"You keep that one. You never know. We might get to watch a little T.V. sometime. If we do, maybe we can share it."

"Deal," agreed Martin.

"Boys, I think one more load from the car will do it. Your swim fins, masks, and beach toys are still in the car. There's a closet by the front door that will be perfect for storing it all."

"Okay, Dad," Benjamin responded. "Come on little brother. Let's get the rest of our stuff and then go check out the pool."

"Sounds good to me, big brother. Let's go."

The boys headed for the car to bring up the last load. Mrs. Kaye was busy unpacking groceries and other kitchen stuff. Mr. Kaye was checking out the beach with his binoculars.

"I think I see dolphins in the water." reported Mr. Kaye. "Come and look."

"In a minute. I'm just getting the drinks in the refrigerator."

"If you don't hurry, you'll miss them."

"Coming," she called.

Mrs. Kaye walked onto the balcony, took the binoculars, and scanned the water. She could see the dolphins surface every few seconds, arching their backs out of the water and then going beneath the water and out of sight. She watched until they were too far down the beach to see. Martin and Benjamin came out on the balcony and were disappointed to learn they had just missed the show.

"Shoot, I bet those will be the last dolphins that swim by here all week," said Martin.

"I think you'll get a chance to see some, too," said Mr. Kaye.

"I hope so," said Benjamin.

"Me too," added Martin.

♐

The rest of that afternoon, Mr. and Mrs. Kaye watched the boys as they went from the ocean to the pool. They were having so much fun going from one to the other, they couldn't believe it when it was time to head up to the condo.

"Already?" asked Benjamin.

"It's time to get ready for dinner," said Mrs. Kaye. "You'll be hungry by the time we're sitting down to eat."

Although the condo had a full kitchen, they planned to eat breakfasts and lunches in the room and in the evening, sample some of the seafood restaurants in the area. Living in the midwest, they didn't get many chances for fresh seafood.

They hurried to get ready and then drove the few blocks to a restaurant they had passed. It was casual but clean and the food smelled delicious. Martin ordered a soft-shell crab sandwich. He did not expect to get what looked like a fried crab, complete with legs or claws or whatever they had, hanging out of the bun. The family got a kick out of the sight and Mrs. Kaye had her camera ready. Martin hesitated for a moment, wondering if he should really try it, but after the first tentative bite, the sandwich didn't last long.

"I wonder how the crab gets soft like that," said Mr. Kaye.

"We'll have to research that question while we're here," said Mrs. Kaye.

Both boys groaned. "Mom, were not here to do research. We're here to have fun," Benjamin pointed out.

"Maybe researching new and interesting things can be fun," Mrs. Kaye responded. "Anyway, I may have to try one of those myself.

"I may have to join you," said Mr. Kaye.

"Can we go swimming when we get back to the condo?" asked Martin.

"If it's not too late," said Mrs. Kaye. "We have to stop at the grocery store and pick up a few things."

Another groan from the boys.

"Why do we have to go shopping on vacation?" asked Martin.

"You'll understand when it's time for breakfast, I expect," Mr. Kaye pointed out.

"But we brought all those groceries. What more do we need?" asked Benjamin.

"Things that wouldn't keep in the car mostly," said Mrs. Kaye. "Milk, eggs, butter, things like that. I want to make sure we have plenty of fresh fruit, too. It shouldn't take long."

Backtracking their route from earlier in the day, they found a grocery store and soon had all the necessary items and some that were probably not necessary, but would be appreciated during the next several days. As they paid for the groceries, Martin looked up and stared in disbelief as a pirate walked through the door.

"Dad, Mom, look." said Martin in a hushed but excited voice, as he patted his father's back to get his attention. "Do you think that's Billy Bowlegs?"

"I don't know, Martin. He looks rather like him. Maybe his pirate ship is parked out in the parking lot," said Mr. Kaye.

"Yeah, I'll bet he sailed on over to the grocery store to buy his crew some travel food. Maybe he's packing a picnic like Mom did this morning," offered Benjamin.

Stepping outside, the boys had the surprise of their lives. There, in the middle of the shopping center parking lot, was a pirate ship. Pirates wandered all around it. When they looked closer, Benjamin and Martin saw it was a float.

Then more floats, all having a pirate theme, pulled into the parking lot. It was the Billy Bowlegs Festival parade, a yearly tradition.

A crowd gathered and cheered when the last float pulled into the parking lot. There, perched in the crow's nest of a great ship flying the skull and crossbones, was the grand marshall of the parade, Captain Billy Bowlegs himself. He was reaching into what looked like a pirate chest and throwing shiny objects to the crowd below. Before the boys could even ask if they could get closer to the float and maybe get whatever he was throwing, two gold looking coins rolled straight for the boys. They each picked one up. Studying them, Mr. Kaye said they were replicas of gold dubloons, the kind pirates might have stolen and buried as treasure.

"Cool," said Martin. "First day here and we've already found pirate treasure."

"It's not real," Benjamin pointed out.

"I know, but it's still cool."

"Yeah, I guess you're right," said Benjamin.

As the parade broke up and the crowd began to leave, Martin said, "I guess we really did arrive on the same day as Billy Bowlegs."

Back at the condo, the boys asked if they still had time for a swim.

"I think that would be fine, boys," said Mrs. Kaye.

"And then can we have a bedtime story?" asked Martin.

"I think that can be arranged," said Mr. Kaye.

A Dangerous Encounter

Billy and his crew sailed into the harbor on a beautiful, clear, summer's day. The men had been in high spirits ever since they finally spotted land. Those who had been on the verge of mutiny were over their rebellious mood, having lost their enthusiasm for conflict after the captain invited them to walk the plank. But now, they were looking forward to some fun on the shores of the Emerald Coast. It was a rough looking bunch that docked and made their way down the gangplank. There was Smelly John walking alongside Captain Bowlegs, leading a crew of about 20 men, each looking more rough and mean than the next. They wore all sorts of colorful clothes and were armed with swords, knives, and guns. They made for quite a sight as they marched along the dock toward town and probably the nearest rum parlor.

"Cap'n, sir, are ya goin ter be givin us our wages so's we kin have our good times in town, if ya take my meanin, sir?"

"I suppose Scully has a point, or they'll be pesterin me for money all night. Give'em part wages, anyway. If we give'em full pay, they'll just be goin broke before the night's over. Ten pounds sterling fer each, and two pounds gold as well. Pay the men, Mr. Smelling."

"Thankee, Cap'n. I expect I'll find good use fer my pay."

Scully was the youngest of the group, no more than 16 years of age, but a hard looking young rough nonetheless. Reaching for the coins Mr. Smelling doled out, he lost hold of a few. Helplessly, he watched as they rolled away from him and slipped between the wooden planks of the dock. A surprised young hand was glad to have been in the right place at the right time and quickly pocketed the coins. Scully walked off with the rest of the mob, muttering about his lost wages.

"Looks like a dern parade, doesn't it," said a boy. He was looking up at the pirates through a crack in the wood.

"Sure does. I guess that one in front with the naval coat is Ol'Billy himself," said another boy.

"Must be," said the first. He was a tall, tow-headed young lad of about 12. He had no shirt or shoes, and his pants, torn off below the knee, were wet from swimming. His companion was a couple years younger, had red hair and...

"Hey that's like me," said Martin excitedly. "Does he look like me, Dad?"

"Don't interrupt him, Martin. It was just getting good."

"That's okay, Benjamin. Actually, Martin, he looked a lot like you, only a little older and he had a darker tan. Both boys did. It was from never wearing a shirt if they could help it," said Mr. Kaye.

"Back then, boys, the ozone layer was thicker and the harmful rays of the sun had a harder time getting through. People didn't worry much about sun exposure," Mrs. Kaye pointed out.

"That's right, so these two boys went almost everywhere with no shirt and barefoot," said Mr. Kaye.

I guess they didn't worry about eating in restaurants with signs that say, 'No shirt, no shoes, no service' either," said Benjamin, grinning.

"No, I guess they didn't," agreed Mr. Kaye. "But something was preying on their minds as they watched Billy and his crew clear the dock, turn down the street, and disappear from sight."

☠

The boys had heard all sorts of stories about the riches to be found in the holds of pirate ships. I guess most boys dream of finding treasure, especially if it seems near at hand. And since Billy Bowlegs was the most successful and enterprising pirate of all, the boys thought his ship might be hard to float for being so full of treasure.

"I'd surely love to see what they've got aboard that ship, wouldn't you, Tap?"

"Sure would, Tip. You think anyone's left to keep an eye on things?"

"Most likely. And if they was as mean and ugly as those that just left, I'd rather not meet'em," said Tip

"If they smelled as bad as that big rascal, I expect our noses would report it if they was anywhere close," added Tap.

☠

"Those are kind of weird names aren't they, Dad?"

"Don't interrupt, Benjamin, it was just getting good."

"Real original," said Benjamin.

"I guess their names do bear some explanation. You see, they went by their nicknames and had for so long they didn't think much about their real names. They had them. But they never got used much."

"So what were their real names, Dad?" asked Martin.

Well, the older boy was given the name of Theodore

Ironhorse. The younger boy was named Thaddeus Arrowfeathers. Their surname was Pettigrew."

"Are they brothers, like Benjamin and me?"

"Yes, they are, Martin," said Mr. Kaye.

"Why'd they have Indian names in the middle?" asked Martin.

"Native Americans. They were Native American names," corrected Mrs. Kaye.

"That's right, boys," continued Mr. Kaye. "And back then, there were lots of Indi – I mean, Native American in the area. The boys' middle names were those of braves who had befriended their parents, at times even fighting with them against hostile white men and natives."

"I still don't get why they were called Tip and Tap," said Martin.

"For the same reason you should have been named Gary Edward Earl," said Benjamin.

"Huh?" wondered Martin.

"Yeah, that way your nickname would have been Geek," Benjamin pointed out.

"Oh, their initials. I get it. Hey!" added Martin.

"Shall we get back to the story?"

"Yeah, Dad, what happened next?" asked Martin.

Well, Tip and Tap couldn't stand the thought of being so close to all that treasure without trying to get a look at it. Slipping into the water, they floated under the dock and around to the far side of the ship. They found some netting the pirates had carelessly left hanging off the side.

Tip whispered to Tap, "I'm gonna pull myself up just so's I can look over the side. You stay here and signal me if you see anything."

Tip slowly climbed, careful not to make a sound. When he got near to reaching the deck, he stepped on something protruding from the side of the ship. With a chill down his spine, he realized he was stepping on a cannon–a big cannon. He could only imagine what it must be like to hear and feel the impact of that awful gun. Lifting himself up and carefully peeking over the side of the ship, he saw no one. "Come on up. It's all clear."

Tap joined his brother on deck. They crouched low so no one could see them from the docks. Figuring the pirates were well into their carousing by now, the boys believed they had plenty of time before anyone returned to the ship.

"Let's look around," said Tip. "I'd sure love to get my hands on some of Ol'Billy's loot."

"Me too," said Tap, "but let's be careful."

The boys slunk across the deck, exploring a pirate ship for the first time in their lives. As they opened a hatch that led to the quarters below, they heard the most awful sound.

"Sounds like someone's choking a mule," whispered Tip. Even though they were taking quite a risk, they couldn't help chuckling when they realized the horrendous noise must be someone snoring.

"If we're real quiet, maybe we can look around a little," said Tip.

"Shouldn't one of us stay up here and keep a look out?" wondered Tap.

"You can if you want, but I think we've still got some time before anyone comes back," said Tip. "I'm heading down."

Tap stayed put as his brother descended the steep stairs that led below decks. Going slowly for fear he would wake up whoever was making that racket, Tip finally reached the bottom of the stairs. The snoring was coming from the front of the ship. He quietly moved in the opposite direction. He passed a few nondescript doors, but felt they were not worth his attention. A large wooden door at the end of the corridor caught his eye. As he got closer, he saw it was gilded with gold. Carved into the door, were images of beautiful mermaids wearing golden crowns and splashing out of the ocean. Below that, an underwater scene showed images of chests filled to overflowing with jewels, silver, and gold. And at the bottom of the door, was an inscription. It read:

Beware good thief, of what doth thee
Lest tread forbidden paths ye
Covet me tender from afar
But eye me tender and you'll be
Restin yer bones at the bottom of the sea

W. A. B.

Tip studied the door, mesmerized by the images and the message before him. If ever there was a door to the inner sanctum of a notorious buccaneer like Billy Bowlegs, this was it. He imagined overflowing chests of treasure like those depicted on the door and pictured coming home to his mother and father with pockets full of gold and jewels. The inscription worried him, though. Captain Bowlegs was terribly jealous of his treasure if he would threaten anyone just for looking at it. Still, the thought of treasure had a powerful allure for Tip, so powerful he stood there longer than he realized.

Tap was up on deck, watching for signs of trouble. He could still hear the snoring sounds coming from below but could neither see nor hear Tip. Afraid to call out for fear of arousing the sleeping pirate, he thought of the signal they used to warn each other of danger. It was a kind of birdcall – one screech of a screech owl and two hoots of a hoot owl. Tap was getting so nervous he decided to try signaling his brother. No one loved adventures more than Tap, but he'd never been on a pirate ship before and he was beginning to think he'd had enough adventure for one day. He gave the signal and waited a few seconds. He gave it again, this time a little louder. He waited for a frightfully long time, but still there was no sign of Tip.

"Are the pirates coming back, Dad?" asked Martin. He had been trying to be still but couldn't restrain himself any longer.

"Martin, let him tell the story," said Benjamin.

"I know, I really tried to wait, but I was getting sca – er – curious," Martin explained.

"I'm sure Tip and Tap will be fine, Martin," said Mrs. Kaye, staring pointedly at Mr. Kaye. She was beginning to think her husband was laying it on a little thick and frightening the boys too much. She also wondered if Mr. Kaye was getting as wrapped up in this adventure as Tip was and forgetting about the time. She didn't want them staying up too late or having nightmares.

"Let's continue and see what happens," said Mr. Kaye.

Tap decided to try one last call. He was just starting to give the signal when he realized he heard something, or rather, heard nothing. No snoring. As he was wondering what that could mean, he did hear something – footsteps. Someone was walking down below and seemed to be heading toward the stairs. Tap hoped it was Tip coming in response to his signal. But when he peeked down the steps, he saw someone, but it wasn't Tip. Looking around for somewhere to hide, he spotted a group of pirates slowly making their way up the dock toward the ship. He ducked behind a barrel, just in time to avoid being discovered by the man coming up on deck. The pirate looked as if he had just woken up. His hair, what there was of it for he was bald except for a thin fringe ringing his head, stuck out in all directions. He staggered as if he had been drinking. In fact, he staggered right toward Tap's barrel. As it happened, Tap had hidden behind a barrel of fresh water. The pirate helped himself to a drink. Tilting his head back and gargling, he made such a funny noise Tap almost laughed out loud. The pirate didn't see Tap, who hugged the other side of the barrel, doing his best to stay out of sight. He watched as the pirate walked to the stern and looked over. The crew moved slowly up the dock. Just then Tip appeared at the top of the stairs. Tap caught his eye, and, putting a finger to his mouth to signal silence, pointed to where the pirate stood, one foot on the ship's railing, looking down at the water.

Acting quickly, Tip motioned for Tap to follow him. They crept up behind the pirate who was being asked to let down the gangplank. Tip realized he had to act quickly if he and Tap were going to escape. The man on deck was just spitting out the water he had gargled, when Tip rushed forward, pushing him as hard as he could. The pirate balanced on the edge for a moment and then plunged into the sea, in full sight of the crew below. Even before he hit the water, the boys ran full speed to the far side of the ship and dove overboard. With all the noise the pirates made laughing at the man splashing about, no one heard the boys enter the water.

They swam under the ship and came up under the dock, near the spot where they had watched the pirates earlier. They stayed long enough to hear the pirates accuse their friend of drunkenly falling over the side on his own. His insistence someone or something had pushed him only brought more laughter and the suggestion that next time he spend less time with the bottle and more time on watch. After all, who could have pushed him?

Tip and Tap carefully slipped away, swimming quietly under the dock until they were a good ways from the commotion of the pirates. They could hear grumbling as one man was ordered to climb the side of the ship and let the gangplank down for the rest of them. When they had floated several hundred yards down the beach, away from danger, Tip and Tap heard a terrible shout of anger.

"Wonder what that was," said Tap.

"I have a pretty good idea. I'll tell you when we're at home safe and sound."

The boys swam to shore and walked up the path from the beach that led to their home. They lived in a clearing, surrounded by creeks, ravines, and dense trees. No other settlers had made their home near them. Even after the long hike, the boys arrived home as excited as ever about their adventure. Tap asked Tip what he thought had happened on board the ship to cause someone to shout so loudly they could hear it all the way down the beach.

"It was almost as if it was enchanted, Tap. I couldn't take my eyes off it. It's a good thing I realized you was signaling me, because I ain't sure I could'a done anything but keep staring at that door. When I finally recognized your signal, I was able to come to my senses again. I opened the door. It was the captain's quarters, all right. I looked around quickly and my eyes happened to catch a glimpse of this."

Tip pulled from his pocket a diamond necklace. It was the fanciest, most beautiful thing either boy had ever seen or imagined.

"There must be a hundred diamonds on that thing," said Tap.

"It was sitting on top of a table by the bed. I grabbed it

and got out of there in a hurry. I tried to close the door back but somehow it kept opening. Must have been some trick to it. Anyway, Billy will know someone was in his cabin tonight. I guess the shout we heard was him discovering the necklace gone. Must'a been a favorite of his, judging by the way it was right there by his bed. I expect that bald old pirate's story about being pushed overboard will get more attention now."

"Aren't you afraid Billy will come after you?" asked Tap. "You know what the inscription on the door said."

"I don't figure he'll know where to look for it. And anyway, I don't believe in superstitious nonsense. He was just trying to scare people off with that message on the door."

"I think it would'a worked on me," said Tap. "What are you gonna do with the necklace?"

"Probably give it to Ma. I'll wait awhile, though. I don't want to scare her by telling her how I got it. Maybe I'll wait till Captain Bowlegs sets sail out of here."

"Good idea," said a sleepy Tap. "I'm gonna sleep well tonight."

"Me too," said Tip. "Adventures have a way of wearing me out."

"Goodnight."

"Goodnight," answered Tip.

As the boys were about to drift off to sleep and dreams of battling pirates and discovering endless piles of pirate loot, Tap remembered something else.

"Oh yeah, I forgot about these." He removed his hand from his pants pocket. In it, were two gold coins.

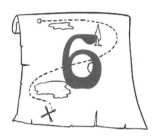

A Day of Dolphins and Other Creatures

It looked like a perfect day. The sky was blue, the water deep green, and the boys couldn't wait to get out there. Because the sea was calm, the boys decided it would be a good day for snorkeling. They planned to explore the ocean floor.

Before they could get out there though, they had to eat a good breakfast.

"It's the most important meal of the day," reminded Mrs. Kaye.

"Did anyone dream of pirates?" asked Mr. Kaye.

"Dream? How can you dream if you're not asleep. And how could anyone sleep with all the snoring Benjamin was doing last night?" asked Martin.

"I wasn't snoring," replied Benjamin.

"Yeah, well, if you weren't snoring, then someone was choking a mule."

Benjamin decided not to argue. After all, he had gotten an especially good night's sleep. And anyway, his snoring wasn't really a problem for him, even if it was for Martin.

Mrs. Kaye surprised them when she said, "I dreamt about pirates."

"You did?" asked Martin.

"Pirates were after me all night. But every time one of them was about to get me, Tip or Tap, or one of you boys would come out of nowhere to my rescue. You would sword fight the pirates until they got scared and ran away. I kept getting confused which were my boys and which were Tip and Tap. You all looked alike. I sure was glad you were around to rescue me."

"Yep, that's what I'm talking about," said Martin. "If any old pirates come after us, I'll take care of'em."

"Thank you, Martin. I know I'll feel safe at the beach today knowing you're around to save me if I should need it."

"No problem, Mom."

"Can we go to that Animals of Florida show today?" asked Benjamin. Mr. and Mrs. Kaye noticed Benjamin didn't poke fun at his younger brother's boasts about handling the pirates. It wasn't necessarily like him to miss that kind of opportunity.

Mrs. Kaye smiled, put her hand on his head, and asked, "Is that what you would like to do today?"

"That's not all I want to do, but it would be fun."

"What does everybody think of that idea?" asked Mr. Kaye.

They all thought it was a great idea. Mrs. Kaye had a brochure about the attraction she had picked up in the office as they were checking in. Looking at the show times, they agreed two o'clock would be perfect. They could be at the beach or the pool all morning. Then, during the hottest part of the day, they could come in and have lunch before attending the show. They all looked forward to that afternoon. But they had some serious fun to have before then as well.

After breakfast, the boys got on their bathing suits. They aimed to dress like Tip and Tap as much as they could.

Mrs. Kaye did insist on shirts at breakfast, and they could count on having to wear shirts to lunches and dinners, too. But she let the bare feet slide. And as soon as breakfast was over, the shirts came off fast. Mr. and Mrs. Kaye each helped a boy with sunscreen and then got themselves ready. Martin and Benjamin gathered the snorkeling gear. Mr. and Mrs. Kaye grabbed their books and they were off to the beach.

As their parents settled into their chairs under the umbrella, Benjamin and Martin lost no time getting on their snorkeling gear. They explored near the water's edge for a long time, frequently popping their heads up and trying to tell their parents what they could see.

"Take your snorkel out so we can understand you," Mrs. Kaye would say to whichever boy was telling them about his latest discovery. After about an hour, Mr. and Mrs. Kaye had quite a pile of sea treasures building by their feet. The boys had discovered several sand dollars, a small conch shell, countless broken shell pieces, and a dead minnow. The boys were equally excited about each find.

For a while, they had been trying to catch some of the thousands of live minnows that swam all around them. Some other kids down the beach had a net with a wooden handle and seemed to be having some success catching minnows.

"Can we get a net like those kids have, Mom?" asked Martin.

"I don't see why not," she replied, reaching into her bag for money. Next door to their condominium was a convenience store. She told them they could walk to the store and see if they had one. The boys dropped their snorkel equipment in front of their parents and began walking.

"I love to see them getting along so well," Mr. Kaye observed.

"So do I. They really are good friends, even if they forget it from time to time."

In a few minutes, they were back, Martin holding a brand new net. Benjamin was a good sport, letting his brother have the first turn. The boys proceeded to wreak general havoc upon the minnow population of the Emerald Coast. Even with the net, they only occasionally caught one. Minnows are fast and apparently accustomed to dodging around things like nets and little boys. When one of the boys did catch a minnow, they would examine it for a short time and then let it go. Mr. and Mrs. Kaye took turns keeping an eye on the boys as the other read.

After awhile, the boys wanted to swim in the pool. Mr. Kaye went with them, leaving Mrs. Kaye alone at a particularly crucial part in her book. The boys wanted to show their father the tricks they could do underwater. No matter what acrobatic feats the boys thought they were doing, it all amounted to about the same thing from Mr. Kaye's perspective. A foot or two would stick out of the water for a few seconds, wave around a little, and then disappear under the water, followed by a head bobbing up, sputtering, and saying something like, "Did you see that one, Dad?" or "That was a good one, wasn't it, Dad?" Mr. Kaye was equally enthusiastic about each stunt and enjoyed watching the boys have fun. Eventually, he joined them in the pool and they had a great time, splashing, diving, and playing blind man's bluff in a corner of the deep end.

A little while later, Mrs. Kaye came to the pool and told everybody she was heading up to the condo to make lunch.

"Do you want me to help?" asked Mr. Kaye.

"That's alright. I'll make lunch today. I'll call you when it's time to come in. It won't take long."

When lunch was ready, she called from the balcony off the boys' room. "All hungry Kaye men report for lunch."

Mr. Kaye and the boys toweled off and headed up to the room. Mrs. Kaye was just setting out a nice spread of sandwiches, fresh fruit, and milk as Benjamin, Martin, and Mr. Kaye came to the table. Mrs. Kaye was pleased to note she didn't have to remind them about their shirts.

"I've never seen real live dolphins, have I, Mom?"

"I don't think so, Martin."

"I wonder if we'll get to touch them," said Benjamin.

"Yeah, that would be sweet. I hope we do," said Martin. "Do you think they'll feel slimy, like those minnows we caught?"

"I don't know. I've never touched one," said Mr. Kaye. "I hope we get to, too."

After lunch, they headed down to the car with Martin and Benjamin asking questions and guessing what they might see at the show. After only a short drive, Mr. Kaye parked the car and the family headed to the front gate. The boys immediately discovered a souvenir shop in the lobby. They had a few minutes before the show started and the boys scoped out a few things they might want as keepsakes from their vacation.

"Benjamin, come here. Look what I found."

"Oh, cool," said Benjamin, looking at a replica of a treasure map Martin held. "There's a place Billy Bowlegs buried his treasure."

"I wish we could find that."

"Same here," agreed Benjamin.

"Boys, lets go on in. We can look more on our way out."

"Okay, Mom," said Benjamin. Then, turning to Martin, he said, "Maybe we can buy that map and figure out how we really can search for treasure."

Entering the arena, they saw lots of bleacher seats, configured in a half circle around a huge pool. The boys were excited to see two dolphins swimming leisurely in the water.

"Hey, there's a soccer ball in the water," noticed Martin, turning to get his parents' attention.

No sooner was that said, than the soccer ball hit Martin in the side of the head.

"Hey, who did that?" Martin instinctively looked for his brother. But Benjamin had a basketball in his hands and was looking down into the pool at one of the dolphins. Martin watched as Benjamin tossed the ball into the pool. Immediately, the dolphin reacted to the ball. He caught it on his nose and tossed it right back into Benjamin's hands.

"Cool!" said Martin. That gave him an idea. He threw the soccer ball toward the second dolphin. The dolphin quickly swam under it and "headed" the ball back to Martin. Martin headed it back to the dolphin and the two of them quickly became engaged in seeing how long they could keep the ball going between them. Martin couldn't believe how quick and agile the dolphin was. He also couldn't believe the dolphin had picked him to play with, even if he didn't exactly like the way he was "picked."

Then, an announcer entered the arena.

"Ladies and gentleman, boys and girls, please take your seats as the greatest dolphin show on earth is about to begin!"

The dolphins swam to the side of the pool, depositing the balls by the announcer. Then they were off, doing incredibly fast laps around the pool and making great leaps out of the water, side by side.

The boys hurried to where their parents were seated.

"Did you see that? Wait till I tell the guys on the team I played headers with a dolphin."

"That dolphin was pretty good, Martin. Maybe he could play on your team," suggested Mr. Kaye.

"Yeah, the field would have to be awfully wet, though." Benjamin was equally pleased to have played basketball with a dolphin.

"That was so cute the dolphins wanted to play with you two," said Mrs. Kaye. "Benjamin, weren't you surprised when he threw you the ball?"

"Sure was. That was so bad."

"Meaning good, of course," said Mr. Kaye.

"Of course," agreed Benjamin.

The show started and the dolphins proceeded to amaze the audience with their grace and intelligence. They made huge, high leaps through hoops and over outstretched wires. They made dancing movements in the water and seemed to sing along to the music that was played over the loud speakers. Each boy had his personal favorite. The dolphin that played catch with Benjamin was a large bottle-nosed dolphin named Bubba. Martin's header partner was a smaller blue dolphin named Lucy.

After the show, the dolphins stayed by the edge of the pool and anyone who wanted could pet them. Benjamin and Martin were among the last to have their turns. They each petted their favorite and, afterwards, Martin was certain Lucy had known he was the one she played soccer with and insisted she winked at him. Benjamin didn't miss the opportunity to point out maybe Martin wanted to go steady with the fish.

"A dolphin is a mammal, Benjamin," said Mrs. Kaye.

"Oh, yeah. I guess that makes her and Martin almost the same species."

Martin was up to the teasing. "At least she's prettier than your girlfriend, fish breath."

The crowd moved on to a smaller arena and were delighted with the antics of several sea lions. Their acrobatic

47

feats were a match for the dolphins. When the show was over, the audience could wander around the grounds and discover exhibits that showed alligators, penguins, and stingrays.

The final exhibit was surprising to the boys. All the others showcased animals associated with the sea. But here was a natural habitat setting with two beautiful, large cats.

"Wow, look at those lions," said Martin.

Mrs. Kaye was studying an information board. "It says here those cats are jaguars. 'These large felines were once a common sight in this part of Florida. Now, because of expansion of cities and neighborhoods, the jaguars' habitat has been almost eliminated,'" she read.

"You mean these guys used to roam wild around here?" asked Martin.

"That's what it says," said Mrs. Kaye.

'I'd sure hate to run into one of those in the woods. He might have me for dinner."

"He'd probably spit you out. You probably taste terrible," said Benjamin.

"I hope so," said Martin.

When the family finished seeing everything, they exited back into the gift shop. Benjamin and Martin decided to split the cost of the treasure map. By the time they filed out of the gift shop it was about dinnertime. They decided to try out a seafood restaurant close to the dolphin show.

As they waited for their food to arrive, Martin said, "I wonder what Tip and Tap will be up to tonight."

"We'll just have to wait and see," responded his father.

"I think the stories have been so much fun," said Mrs. Kaye. "I am wondering about a few things, though."

"Like what?"

"Well, for one thing, do those boys go to school?"

"I hadn't really thought about it, to tell you the truth," admitted Mr. Kaye. "Why do you want to know?"

"Well, I'm concerned about their grammar. They seem to use a rather rough form of speech and if they went to school, perhaps they could learn to speak more properly."

"Jeez, Mom, get real. That's how people in the old days talked. Tip and Tap don't need to go to school."

"I'm not so sure I agree with you, Benjamin. But I suppose it is just a story."

"Yeah, and I think it's cool if they don't go to school. They're lucky," added Martin.

"What else are you wondering about," asked Mr. Kaye?"

"I wonder about their parents."

"What about them, Mom?" asked Martin.

"Well, where are they and how do they feel about their boys just wandering around all by themselves and getting mixed up with pirates? They're just little boys for heavens sakes."

"Back in those days people grew up faster. Maybe Tip and Tap were used to being on their own a lot," suggested Mr. Kaye.

"I still think they would need some supervision, not to mention someone cooking their meals for them and washing their clothes. And what about tucking them in at night? Who's doing that?"

"Mom, it's a story. Everything doesn't have to make sense. Having parents around would ruin it," said Benjamin.

"I beg your pardon," said Mrs. Kaye.

"You know what I mean, Mom. It's just more fun this way. They can stay out late, do whatever they want, and just, you know, make their own decisions about things."

"I suppose you have a point, Benjamin," said Mrs. Kaye.

"But I think it would be nice if they had someone to take care of them."

"Any other concerns?" asked Mr. Kaye.

"Yes, and I suppose you'll all think me terribly silly for wondering, but I can't help it."

"What is it, Mom?" asked Martin.

"Well, what do you boys think of the fact that Tip stole that necklace?"

"What do you mean?" asked Benjamin.

"I wonder if you boys think Tip was right or wrong to steal it?"

Benjamin wasn't sure he was getting it. "Mom, are you saying stealing is wrong and Tip shouldn't have taken the necklace?"

"I'm asking if you boys have thought about that."

"Mom, he's a pirate. He probably stole the necklace. It's okay to steal from a pirate."

"Why is that, Martin? Why isn't stealing from a pirate just like stealing something from a store?"

While Benjamin considered the question, Martin was quick to reply.

"Cause it isn't, that's why. Everybody knows it's okay to steal from a pirate."

Mr. Kaye remained quiet, listening to the conversation with interest. Leave it to his wife to find the social value in discussing a bedtime story about pirates.

"What if the necklace wasn't stolen? Would it still be permissible to steal something that wasn't already stolen?"

"Mom, your thinking way too much about this. It's a story – about a pirate – a bad pirate – a really, really, bad pirate. What's the problem?"

Martin thought the issue was so clear it didn't even need to be discussed. Benjamin, however, was beginning to think about the issues his mother was bringing up a little more seriously.

"I guess if Billy bought the necklace, then it wouldn't be okay to steal it," reasoned Benjamin. "On the other hand, he is a pirate. He's gotten away with doing all sorts of bad things. Maybe he deserves whatever he gets."

"Those who live in glass houses shouldn't throw stones."

It was just like Mom to say something like that, thought Benjamin. He understood his mother was making the point it wasn't up to him, or to Tip and Tap either, to judge someone. Martin was less clear on the point his mother was making.

"Who would throw stones at their own glass house? What does that have to do with taking pirate treasure if you can get your hands on it?"

"Someday you'll understand," she said. "In the meantime, I think you boys should consider whether something is right or wrong, even if it is just in a funny story."

The boys were saved from having to respond by the waiter. He brought a large tray of delicious seafood delicacies. There were broiled sea scallops on rice and a cup of seafood gumbo for Mr. Kaye. Mrs. Kaye had a plate of fried shrimp and hush puppies. Benjamin had grilled amberjack, and Martin decided to try the soft-shell crab sandwich again.

"I think you like the way it looks as much as you like the taste, Martin," said Mr. Kaye. "How is it?"

"Iss goob," said Martin, with his mouth full. "I mean, it's good," he said, after swallowing.

"Benjamin, how was your meal?" asked Mrs. Kaye.

"Real good," answered Benjamin. "Can we swim in the pool when we get back to the condo?"

Back at the condo, the boys ran up and quickly climbed into their swimsuits. Mr. and Mrs. Kaye found chairs close

51

enough to watch the boys swim, but not too close. They didn't want to get splashed by the cannonball jumps the boys liked to perform from the side of the pool.

That night, they had the pool to themselves and enjoyed every inch of it. When it was time to get out, the boys were only a little disappointed. They were looking forward to the bedtime story, so leaving the pool didn't seem so bad. On the way up to the room, Martin wondered if Tip and Tap would run into Billy Bowlegs, face to face.

"I wouldn't want to be in Tip's shoes, I mean bare feet, if Cap'n Billy finds out he stole that necklace," said Martin.

"Neither would I," agreed Benjamin. "I wonder if Tip and Tap will ever get anymore of Billy's treasure."

"I hope so. I think it's fun to steal treasure from a pirate. And who would build a house out of glass, anyway?"

"Never mind, Martin," said Benjamin.

The boys got ready for bed and waited for the story to begin.

"Make it good, Dad," said Martin.

"Yeah, lay it on thick tonight," added Benjamin.

"Real thick," said Martin.

And Mr. Kaye began to tell one of the scariest stories Benjamin and Martin had ever heard.

Bowlegs Wrath

Billy's crew had seen him in plenty of skirmishes and tight spots. They had seen him attack, scuttle, and plunder countless ships. But they had never witnessed a rage such as this. The men were laying low in their quarters and listening to great ranting and raving coming from the Captain's cabin.

"Me diamonds. How could me diamonds be missin? Mr. Smelling, bring me that snuffle snortin oaf. I mean to make him pay for this, I do."

"Yes, sir, Cap'n." And off went Smelly John to fetch a very remorseful and frightened Mr. Gruntee, for that was the name of the unfortunate crewman who had been on watch when the theft occurred.

When Smelly John entered the crew's quarters, Mr. Gruntee meekly followed him out of the cabin, toward his meeting with the Captain.

"Is he awful mad, John?"

"Powerful mad."

"What's he a'mind to do?"

"Haven't a notion, Gruntee, but I doubt yer in fer a promotion."

"Weren't nice of'em to call me them names, even if he is mad."

"What names?" Smelly John asked.

"I heard him call me a snuffle snort or some such."

"Mr. Gruntee, ya have to admit you've been told a'fore ya make one terrible racket in yer sleep," Smelly John felt obliged to point out.

"Well I can't help how I act in me sleep now, can I?"

"Sure wish ya could. We'd all sleep the better for it."

Smelly John figured Mr. Gruntee was keeping the conversation going to put off his meeting with the Captain as long as possible. "We best get on, then."

They arrived at the Captain's door and Smelly John gave a knock.

"Come in," barked Bowlegs.

Opening the door, Mr. Smelling coaxed Gruntee into the room. He was so scared he began to jabber uncontrollably.

"Evenin Cap'n sir and a fine evenin it is, if I do say so myself, which I just did, as I notice. I expect you'll be wantin an explanation fer the terrible loss of yer fine diamonds, not that I seen'em, but I'm sure if they was yers, Cap'n, then the finest'a diamonds they must'a been, or must be, as I'm sure they're somewhere, though we don't exactly know where, which I guess is why we're here and all. Now I've been thinkin about the crook what took'em, sir, and near as I can recall from being pushed overboard – and I'm willin to fergit the part nobody believed me when I said I was pushed – I'll not hold that against anyone, even if they thought I was drunk and not doin me job, which I wasn't, referrin to being drunk, that is. I expect that crook what pushed me was a big'un, unnatural big. Mean and sneaky too, I'd say. Why, I was waylaid by the worst kind of desperate character, what with him havin the gall to board yer ship and go right into yer cabin, where I've never been until just right now and I must say 'tis a fine cabin and very befittin a man of yer stature and understandin nature and all."

Mr. Gruntee stopped dead. He stopped because Captain Bowlegs suggested he stop. He suggested it two ways. For one, he said, "Stop that blatherin right now, or it will be the last you'll ever blather." He also drew his dagger and held it to Mr. Gruntee's throat. The second suggestion wasn't really necessary, but it did drive home the point.

"Now Mr. Gruntee, I wonder if you would be so kind as to explain to me just how it is me diamonds have come up missin."

"I uh, well, sir, Cap'n, I can't say as I actually completely know exactly how such a thing could'a happened, sir."

"Ya don't know?"

"No, sir, 'ceptin I figure he must'a been a great big bloke, a fearless scoundrel, not to mention sneaky, a fact which I believe we've already established, and…"

Billy pressed the dagger a bit more firmly against the man's throat.

"As I was sayin, no more of yer blatherin."

"Yes sir, Cap'n, sir. Blather I will not."

Smelly John thought the Captain was reaching the end of his patience. He feared what might happen next but dared not defend Mr. Gruntee for he had no wish to draw the Captain's wrath himself.

Billy continued his questioning. "Can you tell me, Mr. Gruntee, what exactly you were doin while this large sneak of a scoundrel was helpin himself to me jewels?"

"Well, sir, I, well, ya see, sir, respectin yer position on blatherin and all, I'm afeared to go on and tell ya the whole gist of it, due to yer understandable impatience with such as blatherin."

"MR. GRUNTEE!" yelled Billy. Then, in a voice so soft it scared poor Gruntee all the more, said, "You were asleep at yer watch, weren't ya?"

"Well, sir, no, not entirely, that is. I was awake when I was pushed overboard by that rascal, I sure was awake then, sir."

Mr. Gruntee looked pleased, as if he had made a good accounting of himself under very trying circumstances.

Lowering the dagger and easing Mr. Gruntee's mind considerably, Billy said, "Mr. Gruntee, you are an idiot – an idiot and a dolt. While you was drivin pigs to market so's everyone in the vicinity would know you was sleepin and off yer watch, someone waltzed in here and had their pick of me treasure. And you can be sure, Mr. Gruntee yer lucky I'm only dockin yer wages till you've given me the value of that necklace, which is considerable. The next time I'll not be so good natured. I'll take it outa yer hide!"

With that, Captain Bowlegs turned his back on the two men. John took the opportunity to get himself and Gruntee out of there. Once safely outside the cabin, Mr. Gruntee took a deep breath. "I don't never want to go through that again."

"Ya better hope ya don't have to."

"And I'll be ten years without wages payin off them blamed stones."

"Dad, what were Tip and Tap doing?"

"I was just getting to that, Martin."

"Oh, okay. And, Dad, was Cap'n Bowlegs really going to slit Mr. Gruntee's throat?"

"I expect he was just trying to scare him, Martin."

"Yeah, that's probably what he was doing. And one more thing, Dad?"

"Martin, shut up so he can tell the story."

"It's okay to ask questions, Benjamin. And don't tell your brother to shut up."

"But – oh, alright."

"What was it you wanted to ask, Martin?" asked Mr. Kaye.

"What was that part about driving pigs?"

"It means Mr. Gruntee was snoring loudly, it's an expression," explained Mrs. Kaye.

"Oh, that's a good one. I can't wait to tell my friends Benjamin drives pigs to market every night."

"At least I don't smell like one," said Benjamin.

"That's what you think," Martin replied.

"Let's get back to the story, shall we?" said Mr. Kaye.

Tip and Tap had a hard time getting to sleep after their close call the night before. By the next morning, they were eager for another adventure.

"Maybe we can spy on the ship today and see what they're up to. They say whenever Billy comes to port, it's for three reasons: to let his crew blow off some steam for a few days⬜ to take on supplies for their next voyage⬜ and to find a place to bury a chest of treasure for safe keeping."

"What're you suggesting, Tap?"

"I thought we might see if we can follow them if they go to burying anything, so's we can help ourselves to the goods when they leave it."

"Sounds good to me. Let's get moving."

The boys cleared the table and took a few minutes to wash the dishes before heading out.

"It's nice to see someone taught those boys good manners and habits of cleanliness," interjected Mrs. Kaye.

"It was mostly the raccoons coming in when they was,

I mean were, when they were gone and making a mess of the place. So they took to cleaning up after themselves and putting things away."

"I see," said Mrs. Kaye.

"Anyway," Mr. Kaye continued, "after they cleaned up, they set off toward the docks to spy on Bowlegs' and his crew's movements."

☠

Tip and Tap knew the trails and passes through the woods like they knew their way around their own kitchen cupboards. They planned to come out of the forest a good way from the docks, then work their way back down the beach toward the ship. If they were spotted, they could easily slip back into the woods and hide. When they reached the beach, they were surprised to see the ship directly in front of them, skimming slowly along the shoreline.

"They're off early this morning. Wonder where they're headed," said Tap.

"Wouldn't be surprised if they're lookin fer a place to lighten their load some," answered Tip. "Look, Tap, can you see something up in the crow's nest reflecting the sun whenever a wave catches the ship?"

"Yeah, what is that?"

"Spyglass, I reckon. Let's get out of sight before they spot us."

The boys took to the woods. They stayed just inside the tree line where they could keep an eye on the ship without being seen. Or so they thought.

"Mr. Smelling," came a shout from above. "Don't know that it's worth note'n, but there's two boys just off the beach what seem to be followin our movements."

"Where, Farsythe? I can't see'em," called Smelly John.

"They've taken to the wood now, Mr. Smelling. Must'a caught a reflection off'n me spyglass and knew they was being watched."

"I don't like no one take'n too close a notice of our actions. Keep an eye while I go notify Cap'n Bowlegs."

"Aye, John."

Even without a glass, Mr. Farsythe could usually make things out from farther away than the rest of the crew. Every few minutes he could catch a glimpse of the boys' movements.

When Smelly John informed Captain Bowlegs of Mr. Farsythe's observation, he was most interested. "Boys, ya say. Two of'em. Well I wonder if they're hopin to get their grubby hands on some of me treasure. Tell Mr. Farsythe to keep a look out for'em, but not to use his glass. I don't want'em to know they're bein watched. I think we'll have some fun with them if they are after me treasure. John, go down to the hold and bring up a small chest. We'll be needin a crew to row the dinghy ashore. Bring four men to join you'n me."

"Yes, sir, Cap'n. What was ya want'n in the chest?"

"Rocks, Mr. Smelling. Plain rocks."

"Sir?"

"It's a trap we'll be settin, not buryin treasure. Tell Mr. Drifter to secure the ship. That's all."

"Aye Cap'n. Good idea, that."

Smelly John went to get the chest and fill it with ballast stones. By the time it was full, he needed another strong man to help him carry it. Ears McGinty helped him tote the load up to the deck and into the dinghy. Mr. McGinty was called Ears due to the unfortunate way his ears stuck straight out from his head. He was a respected member of the crew for his strength, his ability to fight, and his hearing. As well as Mr. Farsythe could see, Ears McGinty could hear. Many was the time at sea Ears would pick up the sounds of another ship, even in the dark of night or thick fog. He had alerted the Captain and crew of looming danger at least as often as Mr. Farsythe, just because he could hear so well.

Smelly John went to round up three more men for their jaunt to shore. He chose Big Pete who really wasn't so big, but he was bigger than Little Pete, whom he also chose. Finally, he chose Mr. Gruntee, not wanting to leave him behind to get into more trouble. As they walked toward the dinghy, Smelly John reminded Mr. Gruntee to be on his best behavior and not to open his mouth if he could help it.

As the men were loading the dinghy with provisions and shovels, John went to get the Captain.

"All's ready, sir."

"Good, Mr. Smelling. I have a feelin we're gonna catch ourselves some thievin young lads today. And if we do catch'em tryin fer me treasure, they'll wish they had never heard of Captain Billy Bowlegs."

Before they set out, Captain Bowlegs ordered Little Pete and Big Pete to lay low in the boat, out of sight of curious eyes that might be spying from the shore. It didn't take long for them to reach the beach. Mr. Gruntee and Ears McGinty jumped out and pulled the small boat the last few yards out of the water and up onto the sugary white sand. As the rest of the pirates piled out, Big Pete and Little Pete stayed on board – hidden.

Billy figured the boys would be watching them as they arrived on shore. When they saw four men get off the boat, and later saw four men head back, they would believe everyone had returned to the ship.

"And that's when they'll have a go at me treasure," he had explained.

But Billy planned for Smelly John and Ears to stay behind and nab them as they went for the chest. Captured, the prisoners would be brought before him on his ship. Then the boys would learn the risks of meddling in the business of pirates.

Tip and Tap had kept a close watch on the movements of Billy and his crew. They could see the handles of what they assumed were shovels and hoped those shovels would soon be preparing a nice resting place for a chest of pirate treasure. Excited – and more than a little scared – the boys lay on their stomachs, peering through the brush as two huge pirates lifted a chest and placed it on the beach.

"Do you see that?" whispered Tap.

"I see it," said Tip trying to keep calm. "Let's follow'em and see what they do. If they bury it, we'll come back after they've gone and help ourselves."

Leaving a bit of provisions for the two men hiding in the boat, Smelly John and Ears McGinty picked up the chest. Mr. Gruntee was left to carry the basket of food, the bottles of rum, as well as the shovels. Captain Bowlegs, of course, carried nothing. With Billy in the lead, Smelly John and Ears following close behind with the heavy chest, and Mr. Gruntee huffing and puffing, trying to keep up with all he was carrying, the small band headed into the woods not far from the water's edge.

Tip and Tap mirrored their movements, always keeping a safe distance. They were careful as ever to stay hidden from the band of pirates, chancing to spy on them just enough to follow their progress. As far as they could tell, the men knew nothing of being followed. They were wrong. Ears McGinty could hear their footsteps, especially when the group stopped and the boys took one or two more steps. He motioned to Captain Bowlegs the boys were following their movements and were not far away.

After awhile, the pirates found a little clearing under a large pine tree. The tree was just like a thousand others in the area. The band of pirates stopped on Captain Bowlegs' orders. Mr. Gruntee was especially happy to put down his load. He was careful not to spill any of the rum. Captain Bowlegs had threatened to make him pay for 100 bottles if he spoiled the first drop.

"Men, this spot looks as good as any. Let's have us a meal and then do the work we came to do."

They sat in the shade of the tree, with Billy perched on the chest. The men made a meal of bread, cheese, and dried meat. A bottle of rum was passed, each man taking a generous swig.

In the meantime, Tip and Tap quietly watched the pirates eat their picnic, wishing they had brought some provisions of their own. It had been quite awhile since breakfast, and that had been hurried because they were anxious to get going that morning. Once or twice Tap's stomach growled so loudly Ears could hear it clearly.

"Alright, men," said Captain Bowlegs, "lets start diggin. We'll not need too deep a hole for this small chest."

Mr. Gruntee and Ears McGinty began to dig. In a short while, they had made a sizeable hole. Smelly John and Ears got down on their knees on either side of the hole and lowered the chest until it settled on the bottom. Mr. Gruntee refilled the hole and smoothed out the dirt. Then, the area was covered with fallen pine needles to camouflage the hole. When they were done, Captain Bowlegs said, "Good job, men. Let's have another go at that rum."

The men sat back down and took their turns with the bottle. As the hot afternoon turned to cool evening, the men dozed off, one by one. Even the Captain slept. Mr. Gruntee was the last to succumb to the drowsy feelings. But finally he, too, drifted off. After a while, his snoring woke everyone. Of course, Captain Bowlegs accused him of sleeping on duty, ignoring that the others had, as well.

"But, but, Cap'n, sir. You was all sleepin. I was the last one to fall asleep, and I tried terrible hard to stay awake due to the last incident and all, and..."

"Mr. Gruntee."

"Yes, sir, Cap'n?"

"Shut up."

"Yes, sir, Cap'n, sir, consider me shut up."

"Now then, let's head back to the ship."

The gang of pirates hiked through the woods and back to the beach. Tip and Tap followed from a safe distance. They knew where the pirates were headed, and, more importantly, where the treasure was hidden. Once they were certain the dingy left the beach, they would go back and claim their prize.

By the time the pirates arrived back at the small boat, daylight was fading into dusk. Poor Big Pete and Little Pete were still lying in the boat. They had fallen asleep too and were sunburned and stiff when they awoke. Captain Bowlegs and Mr. Gruntee got aboard the boat. Ears and Smelly John shoved off. Instead of jumping in, though, they dove under the water as Big Pete and Little Pete sat up. If anyone had been watching from the tree line in the gathering gloom of evening, it would have looked like four men left in the boat. Smelly John and Ears McGinty slowly and quietly drifted down the beach before coming to the water's edge. They lay there awhile, listening. When they felt certain no one was watching, they made their way into the woods.

"Put yer ears to working, Ears. I expect we'll hear those two brats a'fore we see'em."

The pirates made their way to the buried chest. Smelly John looked forward to the looks on their faces when the boys realized all their efforts for the day were for a pile of rocks, and they had fallen into a trap, to boot.

Tip and Tap watched the small boat head for the ship and believed they had all the time in the world to dig up the pirate chest. They talked about all the treasure they were about to help themselves to as they walked. Though he couldn't quite put his finger on it, something was nagging at Tip. While Tap talked about what he planned to do with his share of the loot, it finally came to him. He signaled Tap to be quiet and led him through the woods, away from the line that would lead them to the buried chest. They hurried away in silence, until Tip felt they were far enough away to talk safely.

"What's wrong, Tip?" Tap trusted his brother's instincts and had gotten worried, wondering what could make his brother act like this.

"I've been thinking, and it just doesn't add up. Could Billy know these woods better than we do?"

"No way. What are you getting at?"

"Listen, if you buried something by that tree and didn't get back to it for, say six months, could you find it again?"

"I could if I made a map. Oh – I get it. They didn't do a thing to mark the location."

"Exactly what's been bothering me," said Tip. "What if they saw us following them and figured to lay a trap?"

"I'll bet that's what they've done, Tip. It makes sense. But the boat went back to the ship. I sure thought they all left the beach."

"So did I. But I'll bet somehow they left a few men behind to try and nab us."

"There must not be any treasure in that chest. Why don't we just go on home? Let them wait all night if they want to."

"We will if that's what you want to do. But, I'd like to see if we're right. And if we are, I'd like to let them know they'll have to do better than that if they think they can catch us."

"I'm for it. What are you thinking?" asked Tap.

"Do you remember that cave we found over this way about three months ago?"

"Yeah, it's not far from where that chest is buried."

"Remember what we found living in that cave?"

Smiling, Tap remembered the jaguar that resided in the cave. "As I recall, she didn't cotton to visitors too well."

"Right. What if we allowed any pirates waiting fer us to

think they had us on the run? And what if we ran'em right into that old cat. I guess they would have their hands full then."

"They sure would," said Tap.

The boys set their plan. They made their way to the clearing as quietly as if they were walking on air. Ears and Smelly John weren't far away, and Ears was listening closely. There was no way for the chest to be dug up without making enough noise for him to hear.

The problem for the pirates was Smelly John. The boys got a whiff of him the night before while he walked down the dock. As they approached downwind of the clearing, a trick an Indian brave taught them, every gust of wind carried the distinct odor of the big pirate straight to their noses. They didn't have to see him to know he was there.

As soon as they knew at least one pirate, a great big smelly pirate at that, was waiting to trap them, the boys' plan went into effect. Tap soundlessly left and made his way toward the cave. Tip knew he could count on his little brother to do his part. After giving him a few minutes head start, Tip walked into the clearing, as if he had not a care in the world. In a clear voice he said, "I guess I'll help myself to the good Captain's treasure chest. He'll think twice before he decides to leave any loot in these woods again."

Finding the spot where the chest was buried, he started to dig, ready to bolt at the slightest sound. He figured these men were overconfident and wanted a good laugh, seeing him go to the trouble of digging up the chest and discovering it empty of treasure.

The dirt was still loose so he easily dug down to the chest in just a few minutes. Although every muscle was taut and ready, he was rather enjoying himself. He liked the idea of turning the tables on the pirates. He could almost feel their eyes on him and knew they were ready to pounce

He assumed if there was more than one man, they would be together when they came at him. His heart skipped a beat when he realized two men were coming hard at him, from opposite directions. He was standing near the hole he had just uncovered, and for a second froze, unable to decide which way to run.

Just as the men were about to converge on him, he regained his wits and did exactly the opposite of what they expected. Instead of running, Tip jumped into the trap and onto the chest, ducking low as the two men grabbed for him at the same time. As he disappeared into the hole, they collided with a tremendous clunk of their heads, and fell flat on their backs. While they were holding their heads and moaning, Tip quickly grabbed Smelly John's sword. The two men staggered to their feet, still reeling from the impact. They were leaning over, holding their heads. Tip used the flat of the sword to swat them both on the bottom. They didn't know which part to rub first – their tops or their bottoms. As they came to their senses, the looks on their faces turned from pain to anger. Tip lit out toward the cave.

"There goes the lit'le brat. After'em!" said Smelly John.

While Tip was doing his part, Tap had been busy. His job was to locate the jaguar and rile her up so when the pirates came running, she would be ready to greet them. From a safe distance, Tap tossed rocks toward the cave until he eventually enticed the great cat out. She had just stopped growling at him and was about to turn back to her lair when there came a great commotion in the forest. Tip was just ahead of the pirates. Several times he slowed down, deliberately making noise so they could follow him. When he heard Tap give their secret call, one screech of a screech owl and two hoots of a hoot owl, he pulled himself up in a tree and waited for the fun. It turned out, he picked the same tree as Tap.

The two of them watched as the pirates came almost face to face with the Jaguar. It was dark in the forest at night, so all the men saw was the gleam in her eyes reflecting soft moonlight that filtered through the treetops. And they heard her roar. That was enough. They ran as if the cat was chasing them all the way back to the beach, forgetting about the boys they intended to capture, concerned now only with getting back to the ship in one piece. The jaguar had run just a few steps before seeing she had scared them off. Tip and Tap enjoyed what they could see of the show and sat in the tree until the big cat decided to go back to her den.

"Look what I got, Tap."

"What is it?"

"That big smelly one's sword. I even gave him a taste of it, him and that other big lout."

"Nice souvenir. I think I'll go get one, too," said Tap.

"Where?" asked Tip.

"The chest. Even if it is empty, it's still a pirate chest. Maybe I'll have it filled by the time Cap'n Billy decides he's had enough of the Emerald Coast."

"Ha, and enough of those infamous brothers, Tip and Tap."

"Right," said Martin.

"Martin?" said Martin.

"I mean Tap," said Mr. Kaye.

The boys went back to the clearing to claim their prize. Once emptied, it was easy to carry home. They were tired but the adventures of the day were well worth it.

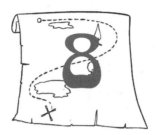

Tresure Ḫunts and Gator's Breath

Mrs. Kaye woke early the next morning. She drew back the curtains and marveled at the panorama of the dawning day. A warm, glowing sun shone in on her sleeping husband. As she slid the door open, she was rewarded by the sound of crashing waves. The sea was rougher than it had been yesterday. *No snorkeling today. But I'm sure the boys will find a way to have fun with those waves*, she thought.

Looking down on the beach, she could see dozens of brightly colored umbrellas set out for the day. One resembled a beach ball, with pretty, wide, pastel stripes. Another looked like a watermelon. Still another bore the colors of the American flag. All in all, the view of the blue-green sea, the sugary white sand, and the umbrellas made Mrs. Kaye feel she had stepped out of her regular life and into a postcard. And the crashing of the waves made it seem like she was in an electronic postcard, complete with movement and sound. "I've been e-mailed to paradise," she said aloud.

"Thanks for sharing the address with me," said Mr. Kaye. Standing behind her, he reached his arms around her and she snuggled against him, holding his hands in her own.

"It's beautiful, isn't it?"

"Yes, it is, and so are you. I believe the sea air agrees with you."

She squeezed her husband's hands a little tighter. They enjoyed the view, feeling the warm sun and the cool breeze. And they knew they were, for all the places they could be in the world, right where they wanted to be, and with whom. The romantic feel of the moment was not lost on Mr. Kaye. For a second, he felt like a sailor, dashing and young, sailing on the high seas with his lady fair, feeling the sea breeze in his hair and the sting of the salty sea in his face. *Wait a minute*, he thought. *The sea breeze fits, but why would I be feeling the sea on my face. I'm two hundred yards away and three floors up.*

Then he heard him.

"OH GROSS! Don't worry, Mom, I'll save you."

Martin, also an early riser, had sneaked out to the balcony from the family room. Armed with a water pistol, his shots were accurate, hitting his father smack in the face. Martin charged his father. "Unhand that damsel in distress if you know what's good for you." He was bare-chested and wore his scabbard fastened to a belt over his pajama bottoms. He approached his mother and father, drawing his sword and preparing for battle.

"Good morning, Martin," said Mr. Kaye, jolted out of his reverie and harshly back to reality. "Good shooting. Your timing leaves a bit to be desired, though."

"Unhand her I say, or it's the cold hard steel of me saber you'll be feeling if you don't."

"You better let go, dear," Mrs. Kaye whispered. "But it was a nice moment while it lasted."

Mr. Kaye unhanded his wife, raising hands high as he did.

"Tis no trouble I'd be wantin from you, good sir. A young rough like yerself would surely make minced meat out'a the likes of me."

"Ah, I see you are wiser than you look, old man," said Martin, pressing his luck a little. "And don't let me catch you treating this lady in such a poor, shabby fashion again, or it'll be all the worse for you."

"Don't worry, I won't let you catch me next time," replied Mr. Kaye.

"What's for breakfast?" asked Martin.

"Let's go see," said his mother.

She and Martin went into the kitchen to prepare the morning meal. Mr. Kaye showered and dressed. He wore a tee shirt and swimsuit, the uniform of the day while on vacation. Breakfast was just being set out when he walked into the kitchen. "Looks mighty good, you two."

"Smells good, too," added Benjamin, who had woken up to the smell of frying bacon and eggs.

"Morning, Benjamin," said Mr. Kaye. "Did you sleep well?"

"Yes, sir, slept like a baby."

"Hope you didn't wet the bed like a baby," said Martin.

"Grow up, twerp."

"Make me, baby."

"Boys!"

"Sorry, Mom, just kidding," said Benjamin.

"Me too," said Martin. "What are we going to do today?" he added.

"We have lots of choices," his mother replied. "What would you like to do?"

"Benjamin and me plan to do some treasure hunting."

"Benjamin and I," corrected Mrs. Kaye.

"You going too, Mom?" Martin couldn't resist the chance to tease his mother.

"I'm going to the beach this morning," said Mrs. Kaye, not rising to the bait. "I'm in a very good part of my book, and I just love sitting by the ocean and reading a good story. What do you all want to do after lunch?"

"How about going to that miniature golf place? It looked like a lot of fun when we drove by it on our way here," said Benjamin.

"Yeah, can we?" echoed Martin.

"I don't see why not. Let's make it a plan," said Mr. Kaye. "Tell me about this treasure hunt."

"Me and Martin – I mean – I and Martin – no, I mean – Martin and *I* have been talking about it. If Billy Bowlegs came to this coast a lot, chances are he really did bury treasure here. And if he did, then we might as well be the ones to find it."

"Right," said Martin. "And we think the sand dunes next door to the condo are a good place to look."

"Why is that?

"It's scientifical, Mom. You know how the water keeps getting closer and closer to the beach all the time, and all that corrosion and stuff, we – well – how did we figure that again, Benjamin?"

"Not corrosion, Martin. *E*-rosion."

"Right, that's what I meant. I still don't get the part about the water getting closer to the beach? Wasn't it always pretty close?"

"Okay, one more time. Long ago, those dunes were farther from the water's edge, but with beach erosion over the years, the dunes have gotten closer to the water, or I guess the water's gotten closer to the dunes."

"So the dunes have moved, but the beach is still right by the water, right?"

"Something like that."

"Very good, Benjamin. How do you know about erosion?"

"School, Dad, don't you think I learn anything there?"

"One can always hope."

"We also remembered you saying how the wind might have changed the dunes over the years, you know, shifted the sand here and there. So some of the low places could have been much higher years ago. If that's the case, we shouldn't have to dig too deep to find treasure."

"Sounds like you two have thought this out very well," observed Mr. Kaye. "Hope you find something."

"Me too," said Martin. "Can we go to the beach now?"

"Lets clean up the breakfast dishes. Then, we'll get sunscreened up and head down to the beach."

In almost no time, the Kayes were ready. Getting sunscreen on had turned into an efficient production, with everyone helping someone cover those hard-to-reach spots. The boys gathered their shovels and buckets and other treasure hunting gear, including the map. They figured it couldn't tell them much, but they thought it might help them find the kind of spot a pirate would choose. The map showed various landmarks pirates liked to use to mark the spot. The boys hoped to use these to find likely places to dig.

Down at the beach, Mr. and Mrs. Kaye settled into their chairs, as the boys set off toward the sand dunes.

"They're so excited about digging for treasure. Imagine if they were to find something. I think they would faint."

"I imagine they would," agreed Mr. Kaye. "They'll have a good time, find something or not."

Mr. and Mrs. Kaye sat and read their books, periodically glancing up and marveling at their surroundings. After awhile, Mrs. Kaye reached into her canvas bag and brought out two ice-cold soft drinks.

"That hits the spot. Thanks."

"You're welcome. Speaking of spots, I wonder if the boys are finding the right spot." "I guess we'll know soon enough," said Mr. Kaye.

"I guess we will," said Mrs. Kaye.

The boys had actually just started digging. Up until then, they had been busy figuring. They carefully surveyed the area and landmarks that would have been there almost 200 years before were noted. What they found was interesting. There was a gnarled old tree with one very strange branch. It came out of the trunk, parallel with the ground, and then turned straight up. The boys knew Native Americans sometimes marked important trails by causing trees to grow like that. But to the boys' minds, it didn't make sense that Native Americans who would have know this area well, would take the trouble of marking a trail this close to the ocean. So, if not Native Americans, it must have been pirates. The boys reasoned the unusual tree was irrefutable proof Billy had used the Native American trail-marking trick to mark the spot. They began to refer to in as "Nat" for Native American Tree.

Two other landmarks got their attention. One looked like part of the sand dunes at first glance. But when the boys investigated more closely, they discovered it was actually a solid white boulder. They thought it unusual for it to be there and wondered if it had been brought to that spot. However it got there, its presence was a powerful sign in Benjamin and Martin's minds. They just knew they were on to something.

The third landmark was more natural. It was a line of sea oats, a kind of wild grass that grew around the coast. The intriguing thing was the plants formed a distinct shape. The boys could see this more clearly when they stood up on the boulder.

"Looks like an axe to me, what do you think, Martin?"

"Yeah, I see it.

"And look, if it was an axe, picture it swinging."

"Looks like it would hit Nat."

"Yeah, and what would happen if the tree were cut down?"

"I'm not sure. What do you think, Benjamin?"

"If it was on the ground, you could walk beside the trunk

so many steps, then turn and follow that branch some more steps, and like that. Sounds like directions pirates might use to mark the spot, doesn't it?"

"Yes," said Martin. "That's gotta be it. Don't you think?"

"It's still a long shot, but who knows. It would make for a good place to hide something and be able to find it again, even if you didn't come back for years."

"So what's next?"

"Let's figure the distances and then pace it out."

"How do we know which direction the tree would fall?"

"We don't, but my guess is the boulder marks the direction," said Benjamin.

So that was how the boys figured where to dig. They went about clearing the sand with their plastic shovels, believing they would strike it rich any second. The work got harder as the hole got deeper. After digging for some time, they stopped to rest and reconsider. They figured the hole was deep enough and even pirates with real shovels would have had trouble digging through the tough soil they were running into now.

"Whaddaya think, Benjamin?"

"I think we would have found something by now if we were in the right spot. Why don't we take a break and go have a swim?"

"Sounds good to me. Let's go."

"Okay, but first, let's camouflage our hole. We don't want someone else getting any ideas."

Back at the beach, the boys found their parents still engrossed in their reading.

"Hi, Mom. Hi, Dad," called Martin.

"Hi, boys, how was the treasure hunt?" asked Mr. Kaye.

"Hot and dry so far," said Benjamin. "But we think we've found markers that could mean something was buried around there. Haven't found anything yet, though."

Mrs. Kaye drew two cold soft drinks from her bag and the boys drank them gratefully. As they quenched their thirsts, the boys related the details of their hunt, including the part about Nat.

"That was good reasoning boys. It sounds like you have gone about this endeavor in a very studied and calculated fashion. Your efforts may yet bear fruit," said Mr. Kaye.

"We're not looking for fruit, Dad,"

"I think you know what I mean, Martin."

"Just kidding."

"You boys look like you could use a swim. I was just thinking of going in and cooling off, myself."

"Yeah, Dad, let's go," said Benjamin as he raced for the water.

"Hey, me too," yelled Martin. Both boys dove right in. They laughed at their father who preferred to wade in, inching slowly into the water.

"Dad, it takes too long to get used to it that way. Just jump in."

"You do it your way and I'll do it mine, Benjamin."

"Suit yourself."

After wading in up to his waist, Mr. Kaye was forced to plunge in the rest of the way. It was either that or be mercilessly tortured by his sons' splashing.

Soon, Mrs. Kaye joined them. The sea was active, the waves crashing all around them. Mr. Kaye showed the boys how to body surf. They were impressed when he caught a ride and made it almost to shore. Benjamin and Martin worked hard to outdo each other. Mr. and Mrs. Kaye joined in the competition. As it turned out, Mrs. Kaye caught the best ride. She seemed to throw herself effortlessly into the middle of a wave and have it pick her up and carry her lightly to shore. The maddening thing, as far as the boys were concerned, was she didn't even care she was winning.

"It doesn't matter who goes the farthest."

"That's easy for you to say," said Benjamin. "You're winning."

"I'm just enjoying the ocean with my family."

After awhile, Mr. and Mrs. Kaye got out of the water and watched the boys work to master the art of body surfing. When the boys finally came out of the ocean, they were tired and hungry.

"You've had a busy morning, boys. Are you ready for lunch?" asked Mr. Kaye.

"I am," said Benjamin.

"Me too," added Martin.

"My turn to make it. I'll call when it's ready," said Mr. Kaye.

As he headed up to the room, the boys talked their mother into watching them in the pool.

"We can show Mom some of our underwater tricks," said Martin.

Mrs. Kaye was treated to several versions of wet, white, feet bottoms, sticking out of the water at various angles. Each time the boys did one of their tricks, she graciously acknowledged their underwater expertise.

"Lunch is served," announced Mr. Kaye from the boys' balcony.

While they ate, the boys told their parents more details of the treasure hunt.

"We must not be digging in the right place," said Martin.

"Maybe," said Benjamin, "but I sure thought the signs were clear."

"Sometimes forgetting about it for a while helps you think about a problem from a different angle," offered Mr. Kaye.

"Your father's right, boys," added Mrs. Kaye. "Let's go play miniature golf. It'll take your minds off the treasure dilemma."

After cleaning up the lunch dishes, the Kayes drove to the Magic Carpet Golf course. They could see this was one of those classic, old layouts, with lots of obstacles to go around, or under, or through, or otherwise avoid, in order to get the ball in the hole.

They each took a different colored ball and a putter. Martin wanted to go first and Benjamin kindly obliged. The first hole, the signature hole of the course, was called the "Magic Carpet" hole. To begin, Martin stood on a fairly large area of green felt and placed his ball on the tee. The fairway had several bumps or mounds to putt over. As soon as he stepped onto the felt, he realized the first ten feet of the fairway bounced up and down.

"I guess this is the magic carpet part," said Martin.

Martin hit his putt hard. The ball bounced off the backstop behind the hole and straight into the hole on the fly.

"Great shot Martin," said Mr. Kaye.

"Thank you, thank you. I'll be glad to sign autographs after the game."

"Gee thanks, pro," said Benjamin. "How 'bout take your bows somewhere else so I can have my turn."

Martin did move. He moved to the edge of the magic carpet and jumped up and down for all he was worth while Benjamin tried to concentrate on his shot. Benjamin was up to the challenge.

"Alright squirt, jump all you want. I'll still make a good shot."

And he did. His ball rolled up and down over the bumps heading straight for the hole. At the last second, Martin gave a tremendous jump, knocking the ball off course by a good foot and a half. Martin was enjoying himself immensely, at least until he saw Benjamin's ball circle in a wide arc around the hole, and then, making progressively smaller circles, eventually drop into the hole.

"Thanks for the help, Martin," said Benjamin.

"How did that happen?"

"I think it went in because Benjamin was such a good sport about all your shenanigans, Martin."

Mrs. Kaye was next. Her putt was a bit off line but turned toward the hole, passed it once, then rolled backwards into the cup.

"Looks like this first hole was designed to maximize the putter's success," observed Mr. Kaye.

"Huh?" wondered Martin.

"I mean, it's hard to miss, don't you think?" said Mr. Kaye as his putt also found the hole.

"It's not fair. I'm the only one who hit a shot straight in."

"Oh you're sooo good," said Benjamin.

"Hey, we'll see who's good and who isn't," Martin responded.

"Let's go on to the next hole, boys," said Mrs. Kaye. "I'm sure you'll both do very well."

The rest of the course was a nice balance of challenging and easier holes. The scores were close. Mrs. Kaye was ahead of Mr. Kaye and Benjamin by one stroke, and Martin was behind by one more shot. As they approached the seventeenth hole, anyone had a chance to win.

The seventeenth hole was an ordinary looking layout, a fairly straight shot, if you could putt the ball between two rocks. To one side, was an opening that looked like a small cave.

"I wonder what happens if your ball goes in there?" said Benjamin.

"You'll probably find out," said Martin. .

"We'll see, little brother. Take your turn."

Martin's ball rolled right between the two rocks and into the cup.

"A hole-in-one! I could still win," said Martin.

"Very good shot," said Mrs. Kaye.

"Especially good under pressure," added Mr. Kaye.

"Lucky," said Benjamin.

Mr. Kaye went next. After his first shot ended up a few inches from the cup, he tapped in for a two. When it was her turn, the boys hoped their mother would mess up. They each wanted to win the match, and this was their last chance to catch her because the eighteenth hole was an automatic hole-in-one. The boys had already checked it out and seen that the object of the last hole was to putt up a gangplank and land your ball in a mug held by a pirate. If you made it into the mug, you won a prize. Even if you missed the mug, you still made a hole in one because your ball didn't come back to you.

So they watched carefully as Mrs. Kaye hit her putt. The ball rolled, as if it had eyes, straight into the hole.

"Aw, shoot," said Martin.

"Good shot. That makes you the winner. Well done."

"Thank you Mr. Kaye. I see we have one good sport here," she said, looking playfully at Martin.

Benjamin took his turn. But because his putt couldn't win the match, he didn't try very hard. The ball caromed off one of the rocks and went right into the cave.

"Doesn't matter much anyway," he said. "Mom already won."

"Yeah, but now I can beat you," said Martin. "If you make two, we tie, and a three puts me ahead. Mom, did you bring your camera? When Benjamin sticks his head in that cave, it may make for a good picture."

"I have it right here," said Mrs. Kaye, pulling, as usual, just what she needed out of her bag.

It was a good thing she was ready because as Benjamin crouched down to look into the cave, a giant alligator rushed out. Benjamin jumped straight up in the air as the jaws opened showing rows of sharp teeth.

"Holy Smokes!" he yelled.

Smoke billowed out, engulfing Benjamin in the gator's breath. His heart pounded as the alligator slowly receded back into the cave. Mrs. Kaye snapped a picture at some point.

"I thought I was a goner."

"I wasn't expecting that," said Mr. Kaye, laughing.

"Me neither," said Martin.

"I hope my picture turns out," said Mrs. Kaye. "It should be priceless."

After catching his breath, Benjamin remembered something. "Where's my ball?"

They were about to go ask for another one when Martin happened to look in the hole. Resting at the bottom was Benjamin's ball.

"Now how'd *that* happen?" Martin wondered.

As they looked into the cup, they saw there was an opening in the side, just big enough for a golf ball to roll through.

"Guess I made a hole in one, too," observed Benjamin.

"I guess you did at that," agreed Mr. Kaye. "Nice shot."

"That's not fair, my shot was much better than yours."

"Martin, be a good sport," said his mother.

"Oh, alright. But it's hard to be a good sport when everybody beats you."

On the final hole, Mr. and Mrs. Kaye failed to get the ball in the pirate's mug. Benjamin tried next, as Martin wanted to be the last to play. Benjamin's ball hit the edge of the mug but didn't go in.

"Must not want to give away too many prizes," said Benjamin.

"I think you're right," said Mr. Kaye. "Let's see what you can do, Martin."

Martin aimed carefully and swung. He had paid close attention to the other putts and knew besides hitting it straight, you had to hit it hard enough to get some lift on the ball as it came off the gangplank. The family watched Martin's ball roll up the ramp and disappear right into the pirate's mug. A bell rang loudly to alert everyone of the hole-n-one.

"Way to go, Martin." said Benjamin.

"Nice shot. I didn't think anyone could make that," said Mrs. Kaye

They took the putters back to the desk and Martin received his prize. It was a gold pirate coin.

"We keep running into fake pirate gold. Maybe that means we'll find some for real while we're here," said Martin.

↗

They had already decided on a new seafood restaurant for the evening.

On the way there, Martin said, "Let's get home early tonight so we can have a long Tip and Tap story."

"Sounds good to me," said Benjamin. "I wonder what Tip and Tap will be up to tonight. I'll bet they'll get the best of Billy Bowlegs and his pirates again."

"I don't know, Benjamin. Tip and Tap have been awfully lucky. Maybe their luck is about to run out."

"What do you mean, Dad? Is something bad going to happen?" Martin asked.

"You'll have to wait and see," said Mr. Kaye.

A Forbidden Visit

Big Pete and Little Pete were back on shore, waiting for Smelly John and Ears McGinty to return with the prisoners. They were restless and impatient by the time they finally saw them coming. Out of breath, it took a few minutes of huffing and puffing and breath catching before the scared men could explain why they were empty handed.

The men rowed back to the ship.

"It's 'appy I am, as it's you, John, and not me, what will be explainin all that to the Cap'n," said Big Pete.

Smelly John wasn't happy about it. Not at all. He knew how poorly Captain Bowlegs took bad news. And Mr. Smelling would be giving him his second helping of it in as many days.

The waves were high and the oarsmen had difficulty getting the small boat out past the breakers. Several times the waves seemed to lift them up and carry them backwards, almost to shore. Eventually, they were able to row hard enough to pass the breaking waves and make it to the ship. By the time they did, though, they were all soaked to the bone, especially Big Pete and Little Pete who had worked up quite a sweat.

The men boarded the ship, and the dinghy was hoisted up and secured. From the ship's deck, Billy silently noted they were returning empy-handed. When the men came forward and Smelly John told his tale, Billy listened without interruption. John and the others waited for the outburst from their captain, but it never came. Finally, after appearing deep in thought, Bowlegs spoke.

"Men, I see we have some clever, and, as Mr. Gruntee will be happy to tell ya, sneaky, thieves on our hands. They've outsmarted us at least once, and I've a strong notion they're the ones what stole me jewels, too."

"Well, all they stole tonight was a box'a rocks, Cap'n."

The crew laughed at the thought of the boys opening the box and discovering ordinary stones, not the precious ones they were hoping to find.

"Aye, Mr. Smelling, rocks and your sword most likely. Or did you decide to make them a gift of your saber?"

In all the confusion, Smelly John hadn't realized his sword was gone.

"Why, the lit'le buggers stole me sword. How do you like that?"

"I don't," said Billy.

"I don't guess I do, neither," said Smelly John, "and I intend to have a strong word or two next time I run into'em."

"They're clever'uns, but they're just lads, no more'n ten'r twelve years, I expect. We should have no trouble thinkin of a way to outsmart'em. If the best and most fearsome thieves on the high seas can't best a couple'a young brats, I'll be hanged."

"What have ya got in mind, Cap'n, sir?" asked Ears McGinty.

"Here's my thinkin, men. What do these boys seem to want?"

"To escape from us, Captain?" offered Smelly John.

"Try again, Mr. Smelling."

"To get us eaten alive by a lion?" said Smelly John, hoping he was right this time.

"No, Mr. Smelling. Think harder."

He tried, but the effort caused an aching between his ears. Smelly John generally gave up on thinking hard long before the aching began. But this time he felt pressured to continue, especially since he had failed to capture the two boys.

Finally, he said, "nothin I can think of, 'cept fer our bounty."

"That's it, Mr. Smelling. They want treasure."

"Why, I s'pose they do," said Smelly John.

"So if we wanted to catch these fish, what bait must we set?"

Smelly John thought it unfair of the Captain to change the subject, just when he was catching on to the conversation. Even as he replied, he had a sinking feeling he was missing something.

"Uh, what type of fish are we after again, Cap'n?"

"Not FISH, Mr. Smelling," bellowed the Captain. "BOYS. We're wantin the boys that's wantin' me treasure."

"Right, Cap'n. That's what I thought in the first place," said Smelly John, relieved they were back on the original topic.

Exasperated, Captain Bowlegs told Smelly John and the rest of the crew that, in the morning, they would be burying some real treasure. "If these lads are as clever and determined as I think they are, they'll follow us. When they do, we'll nab'em. And if it's wild animals they're fond of, maybe they'll enjoy being introduced to Miss Ally."

"Aw, Cap'n, that'd be a terrible thing to do. They're just lads full'a adventure. Ya wouldn't want to be hurtin'em now, would ya?"

"Mr. Smelling, they've stolen me jewels and made fools of us, have they not?"

"They did get the best'a me'n Ears, that's certain, sir.

But I don't know they should be introduced to Miss Ally, just on account'a that."

"Mr. Smelling, are ya goin soft on me, then?"

"No, sir, it's only just that they're boys is all. If they was men and knew what they was gettin into, then I'd not feel in any way sorry for'em. But I'd sure hate to be involved in hurtin children."

"Well, I swear, Mr. Smelling. I always thought ya were mean and cold-hearted as they come. Now I learn you've got a streak'a nursemaid in ya. But, beware, if those boys come lookin fer me treasure, they'll have me saber or the plank as their reward. Do I make myself clear?"

"Aye, sir," said Mr. Smelling, having pushed his luck as far as he dared.

To the rest of the crew, Captain Bowlegs said, "And do I make myself clear to everyone here? There will be no mercy fer the lads when we capture'em. I'll have me jewels returned and see them to their graves. If they are unlucky enough to follow us and learn our secrets, I will have no choice. I'll leave no one alive who knows where I bury me treasure. Dead men tell no tales. And neither do dead lads."

"Aye, sir," responded the rest of the crew in unison.

The next morning, Tip and Tap were more excited than ever about helping themselves to Captain Bowlegs' treasure. Over a quick breakfast, Tip said, "Yesterday they set up a decoy to lure us in and try to nab us. And we weren't careful enough. They knew we was watching. Today will be different. Today we've gotta be more careful."

"I hope we didn't scare'em off," said Tap. "Ever since we watched Billy sail into our harbor, I've imagined finding one of his treasure chests filled to the top with silver and gold and all kinds of jewels."

"Maybe we'll get that chance today. Let's head out to the shore and keep an eye on'em. They got an early start yesterday."

The boys were especially careful making their way to the beach. If anyone was on the lookout, they wanted to spot the lookers before the lookers spotted them. As they approached the shore, they made sure to stay hidden behind the vegetation. They looked for the ship, and there she was, on the move again. The boys watched as the *Tell No Tales* slowly turned away from shore and headed out to sea.

"Looks like they're leaving, Tip."

"Sure does."

"But now we'll never get any more pirate treasure," cried Tap, seeing his dreams of pirate plunder sailing away right before his eyes.

They watched helplessly as the ship continued turning so it was headed directly away from them.

"Dad?"

"Yes, Martin?"

"Billy Bowlegs can't leave yet."

"Yeah, Dad. Billy and his crew have to stay around, don't they?" asked Benjamin.

"Yes, don't they?" added Mrs. Kaye.

"As I was saying..." continued Mr. Kaye.

Tip and Tap thought Captain Bowlegs was sailing away, but then realized he was turning the ship to head back the other way, using the best wind he had to do it. Billy was as respected for his sailing skill as he was feared for his pirating. He knew if he tried to come about toward shore, he would risk scuttling her in the shallows. So, he instructed Mr. Drifter to come about full to port and head up the coastline.

☠

"Oh, okay," said Martin.

"Good," said Benjamin.

"Excellent," added Mrs. Kaye. "We weren't ready to be rid of Ol'Billy just yet, were we boys?"

"No ma'am," Benjamin and Martin answered in unison.

"May I continue, then?" asked Mr. Kaye.

"Of course. Please proceed," answered Mrs. Kaye.

"Okay, let's see. Oh yes. Tap was about to point out the *Tell No Tales*
was coming about and heading back toward the pier."

☠

"Let's follow and see where they go," suggested Tip.

The ship sailed slowly past the pier. Down the coast, there was a collection of several small islands with narrow channels of water between them. The ship was headed straight for them.

The boys did their best to keep up with the ship and stay out of sight at the same time. When the ship passed the pier, the boys were forced to make their way behind the row of storefronts and saloons in the little town. They lost sight of the ship momentarily. They broke into a dead run to pass the town and get to a vantage point so they could continue to observe the ship. When they were past the town and back to the tree line near shore, there was no sign of the ship anywhere. "Must've gone into the islands, Tap."

"I guess they did. Perfect place to bury treasure, if you ask me. They could have all the privacy they need to hide something."

"Except we're gonna be watching them," said Tip.

"Right. Let's go."

Tip and Tap knew these islands well, all except for the island called Mystery Ally. It was unexplored and – well – mysterious. The other islands were plain enough, all looking like much of the Florida coast – white sand and heavy vegetation creeping down towards the shore. But this one was different. The last barrier island, it was covered in a shroud of mist and mystery. No one had ever come back alive from Mystery Ally, or so the story was told. And although their parents trusted them and gave them lots of freedom to roam, they made it clear the boys were never to go there.

"Do you suppose they're headin for Mystery Ally?" wondered Tap.

"I wouldn't be surprised," answered Tip. "That'd be just the kind of evil place I'd expect Bowlegs to go."

"What'll we do if that's where he is?" asked Tap. "You know what Mom and Dad said. We're never to go there."

"I know," said Tip. "But they don't really know why. It's just what everybody says about the place. But why should it be any different from these other islands? There's nothing more dangerous than an occasional shark swimming between them. I'll bet no one knows these islands better than we do. If anyone can handle Mystery Ally, it's you and me."

"Let's just hope that's not where they're headed," said Tap.

Tip and Tap made their way over to the first island quickly. They used sand bars in the channels to get from one island to another without having to swim more than a few hundred feet at a time, a distance easily handled by excellent swimmers like Tip and Tap. They crossed the first island without incident. Then the second and still no sign of the *Tell No Tales*. On the far shore, they found themselves starring across a channel at the mist-shrouded, forbidden island.

"What if the stories are true, Tip?"

"I don't know, Tap. I just know I'm not ready to give up on finding us some pirate treasure. Not yet I'm not."

"I guess I'm not either, Tip. So what's next?"

As the boys contemplated their next move, the pirates were putting their plan in place. They had brought the *Tell No Tales* in as close to the outer bank of Mystery Ally as they could, using a deep channel close to shore. The dinghy was used to transport the treasure chest. But the pirates who were not rowing the boat simply swam a short ways and then waded up onto the beach. Big Pete and Smelly John unloaded the treasure chest when the boat reached the shore.

Heavy, thought Smelly John. *Wouldn't mind having this one fer meself.* He wondered if Big Pete was thinking the same thing. "Where to now, Cap'n?" he asked.

"I want Mr. Farsythe and Ears to be our lookout and 'hearout' fer the lads."

"Yes, sir, Cap'n," responded Mr. McGinty.

"Where do you want us to hide?" asked Mr. Farsythe.

"If they're on foot, they'll likely come through the forest fer cover. So make yer ways inside the tree line on the other shore. Climb trees about a hundred feet apart, so's ya can still see one another. If Ears hears anything or if Farsythe sees anything, signal the other. Then when the boys have passed, follow them. Stay behind'em and we'll take care'a the rest. Just don't let'em by ya if they turn tail and make a run fer it. Best be goin now."

As the men turned to go, Billy included one last instruction.

"And gentlemen, me humor for acceptin failure has run its course. Am I understood?"

"Aye, aye, sir." said Mr. Farsythe and Mr. McGinty.

After they had gone, Captain Bowlegs assembled the rest of the crew. In all, 15 men had come ashore, including the Captain. That left a handful of pirates to man the ship and to be on the lookout for trouble from land or sea. Billy knew better than to leave the ship poorly guarded as he had their first night on the Emerald Coast.

"Mr. Smelling, I want you and Big Pete to pay a visit to Miss Ally. Let'er know she has company in the neighborhood. Keep an eye on her and be able to tell us her whereabouts. The rest of us'll follow along behind with the treasure. I plan to bury it somewhere in Miss Ally's garden. That way, she can keep a nice, evil eye on it fer me. And, when those boys come fer me treasure, they'll find themselves between a rock and a hard place, I'll bet."

Big Pete and Mr. Smelling took off to follow orders. And...

☠

"Hey, Dad?"

"Can't you just let Dad tell the story?"

"It's okay, Benjamin, we'll get back to the story in a minute. What is it, Martin?"

"Well, remember when we first met Billy? Didn't you say this story was about the first time he had sailed to the Emerald Coast?"

"Yes, I believe I did."

"Then how does he know about Mystery Ally and Miss Ally, whoever she is."

"I see what you mean," said Mr. Kaye.

"That's very observant of you, Martin. I didn't catch that at all," said Mrs. Kaye.

"Neither did I," said Benjamin. "Good going, squirt. What should we do about that, Dad?" asked Benjamin.

"Well, to tell you the truth, I forgot I said it was the first time Billy and his crew had ever come to the Emerald

Coast. I guess I said that part because it was our first time coming here and I wanted there to be some similarities in the story to our trip."

"And that was a good idea," said Mrs. Kaye.

"Yeah, Dad, I like it when things we do happen in the Tip and Tap stories," said Benjamin.

"Oh, you've noticed that, have you?" asked Mr. Kaye.

"Sure, like when we went to the Animals of Florida show and saw the jaguars, and then Tip and Tap had that jaguar chase off Smelly John and Ears McGinty."

"Oh yeah," piped up Martin. "And like when we got two pirate coins from the parade, and Tip and Tap got those two gold coins in the story that night."

"And the parade, the parade we saw that night and then when Tip and Tap were spying on the pirates, didn't Tip say something like, 'look at the parade?'" added Benjamin.

"I think he said, 'looks like a dern parade,' or something like that," remembered Martin.

"Dad, you're better than I thought at this story telling stuff," said Benjamin.

"Thank you, Benjamin. But what should we do about this mistake I've made? Should we forget about Mystery Ally if it's inconsistent with the beginning of the story?"

"No, Dad, we've got to see what happens. This is a good part," said Martin.

"Yeah, Dad, Mystery Ally is as much a part of the story now as anything that happened at the beginning."

"Well, then, should we try to fix it or just ignore the story line discrepancy?" asked Mr. Kaye.

"Perhaps the pirates sailed to the Emerald Coast by way of Mystery Ally," suggested Mrs. Kaye. "They could have stopped there first before they docked that first night. Maybe that's how they knew about Miss Ally, whoever she is."

"Splendid idea, Mrs. Kaye. What do you think, boys?"

"That would work," said Martin. "They landed at

Mystery Ally to hide some treasure or something. Then, Tip and Tap spotted the ship coming around from behind the island. I'll bet that's what really happened."

"I'll bet you're right," said Mr. Kaye. He winked at Benjamin who realized but refrained from pointing out that, of course, none of this "really happened." Martin was so caught up in the story, it must seem very real to him. *Good*, thought Mr. Kaye, feeling satisfied his story was being taken seriously.

"Well, then, that is what happened. Now, as I was just saying..."

Big Pete and Smelly John headed into the woods, using a trail beside a little spring that was the start of a fresh water creek leading toward the center of the island. Billy and the rest of the crew waited for them to get a good start, then followed along the same trail. They wanted to make sure Miss Ally was occupied with Big Pete and Smelly John before they trespassed in her neighborhood.

Smelly John and Big Pete were not happy. One close encounter with Miss Ally was all either one of them cared to have – and they had already had it. When the *Tell No Tales* anchored at Mystery Ally en route to docking in Tip and Tap's town, Billy was looking to take on supplies of fresh water.

"Good one Dad," said Martin.
"Thank you, Martin. I try. So..."

Luck had been with them as they found a freshwater spring. But the spring wasn't the only discovery made that day. Smelly John had the misfortune to meet Miss

Ally. She had sprung from the brush while he was bending over, filling a barrel with water. Surprising him, he had no chance to escape as she grabbed hold of his leg and began to slowly but surely drag him into a pond that was fed by the spring. Apparently, that was where she liked to store her food, waiting until she was hungry to enjoy her feast. That's what alligators do, and that's what Miss Ally was – a giant, eighteen-foot alligator. She was the queen of Mystery Ally and had a barbarous way of greeting visitors.

Smelly John had done his best to get away, but Miss Ally was plenty strong enough to pull even a large man like him into the water. But, as she neared the pool, something made her stop and let him go. Smelly John and the rest of the crew who had witnessed the horrifying event watched in shock as the gator turned and plunged into the pond.

"She just spat me right out, she did," said Smelly John after catching his breath and recovering from the ordeal. He wondered aloud what had cause the great gator to let him go, leading Big Pete to draw the obvious conclusion.

"Ya moost taste worse than ya smell, John."

The crew had a laugh at Smelly John's expense. But he laughed along with them, relieved to know the giant gator had no appetite for him.

While Smelly John and Big Pete were heading toward Miss Ally's residence from the south side of the island, the boys, having crossed the narrow channel between the last, familiar island, and Mystery Ally, were entering the woods from the north shore. As they headed deeper into the woods, their fear of the island began to fade.

"What's so scary about this place?" whispered Tap.

"Yeah, I know," said Tip. "Don't know what all the fuss is about. Still, let's keep our eyes peeled and be ready for anything."

But they weren't ready for two pirates in the trees directly above them.

Mr. McGinty and Mr. Farsythe waited for the boys to get out of earshot and then climbed carefully and quietly down from their perches and followed along behind.

Tip and Tap were beginning to feel rather smug about outsmarting Billy at his own game. They fully expected to be coming home tonight with pockets full of pirate treasure. In their confidence, they had all but forgotten the stories of Mystery Ally and the dangers facing anyone who went there. But that was about to change.

Meanwhile, Big Pete and Smelly John had indeed found Miss Ally. The two pirates peered through the brush into the clearing surrounding her pond. She was sunning herself on the opposite bank. The ground was sandy, Miss Ally's own private beach. On the edge of the clearing was an odd-shaped tree. It had...

"Like our tree? Like Nat?"

"I suppose it was a lot like that tree, Martin," responded Mr. Kaye. "That is just the kind of tree it was. And Smelly John and Big Pete knew Captain Bowlegs would think that tree was a perfect marker for burying his treasure."

Tip and Tap continued across the island. In fact, they were about to enter Miss Ally's neighborhood. They stopped to study the clearing before going any further. Because she was on the near slope of the bank, they couldn't see the giant gator. But something about the open space made them think twice about entering. It just felt dangerous.

"Let's slip around to the other side of that pond, Tap. I don't like the feel of this place."

"Neither do I. Let's go."

The boys began to skirt around the clearing when they came face to face with Ears McGinty.

"Hello, boys. Fancy meetin you here."

Tip and Tap were so surprised that, for a second, they froze. They turned to run the other way but ran straight into more trouble. Tip bounced off Mr. Farsythe's chest and fell back into Tap. Both boys tumbled to the ground as the pirates advanced on them. The boys sprang to their feet and, thinking the woods were filled with pirates, ran into the clearing to escape. Maybe they could outrun the oversized rogues. They made it to the clearing and did seem to be leaving the pirates behind. Unfortunately, they ran directly toward Miss Ally, who lurked just below the top of the bank, alert now to the commotion. Tip turned to look over his shoulder to see if the pirates were on their heels. He was just wondering why they weren't being followed as he headed, unknowingly, within reach of Miss Ally. Tap saw her just before she lunged toward his brother. Hurling himself at Tip, he knocked him out of reach of the giant beast. The boys found themselves on the ground again, surrounded by pirates emerging from the brush all around them. And if that wasn't bad enough, a hungry-looking alligator was getting closer every second. Their situation was desperate, for certain. As the giant gator advanced, an unlikely rescuer spoke up.

"Mr. Smelling, grab the young'uns before Miss Ally has'er way with'em. There's still the matter of me diamonds to discuss."

"Aye, Cap'n."

Mr. Smelling walked right between Miss Ally and the boys. It terrified the boys even more to see the big pirate show no fear of the gator. They didn't know Smelly John and Miss Ally had an arrangement of sorts. She remembered getting one taste of him and did not relish having another. When he advanced on the boys, Miss Ally reluctantly backed away, then turned and slipped into the water. Smelly John grabbed Tip and Tap by the arms and led them to Captain Bowlegs.

"Boys, ya shouldn't a'been botherin about me doings. I'm afraid you've a lesson to learn that's more than you bargained fer when ya decided to come after me treasure. You've made fools of some'a me men and I see ya have Mr. Smelling's sword, which you may return to him now." Billy continued as Tip undid the sword from his belt and surrendered it to Mr. Smelling. "But when it comes to outsmarting me, few men have lived to do much braggin about that. Mr. Smelling, see to it these lads are locked in the hold. Make sure they're tied up good and tight. We'll finish our task and join ya shortly."

"Wha, what are you gonna do with us?" asked Tap. He was the first one of the two boys to find his voice.

"Whatever I want, I expect, ya lit'le brat," replied Billy.

"You won't hurt him or you'll answer to me for it," Tip responded, mustering all the courage he could find at the moment.

"I'd not be thinkin I was in a position to make demands, ya insolent young thief. I'll do whatever I want with the both'a ya and I don't expect you'll get much of a say in it. Take'em away men. Maybe being me prisoners will learn ya better manners than to talk back to a Captain."

Sea, Sand, Searches, and Human Kites

When the story ended with Tip and Tap in dire straits indeed, Benjamin and Martin had all sorts of questions. But it was late and their questions would have to wait until morning. Tucking them in, Mr. Kaye told them to get right to sleep.

"Your father's right, boys. We've got another full day tomorrow and you'll need your rest," said Mrs. Kaye.

But through the closed door, they heard Martin.

"How could Dad let Billy and his band of pirates get Tip and Tap? He knows what they'll do to them."

"I heard that," said Mr. Kaye.

"Dad won't let Billy hurt them, Martin. He's just making the story more exciting. You watch. They'll get away from that ship somehow."

"I heard that, too," said Mr. Kaye.

"They better, or Bowlegs'll make them walk the plank," said Martin.

"That's enough, boys. Go to sleep now," said Mr. Kaye.

↗

It grew quiet then. Mr. and Mrs. Kaye enjoyed a bit more of the evening by sitting out on their deck. They listened and watched as the whitecaps crashed, seeming to glow with their own incandescence as they reflected the moonlight from the night sky.

"We can stay here forever, can't we, dear?"

"If forever means three more nights," answered Mr. Kaye.

"Well, I can pretend, at least. This is a good vacation for pretending. You're doing such a wonderful job of ending each day on a high note. Have you noticed the boys haven't once complained about having to go to bed? In fact, they've been eager for bedtime. They can't wait to hear the next installment of the Tip and Tap story."

"I hadn't thought about it, but you're right. They haven't complained about going to bed. And neither shall I. It's been a full day and I am tired."

"Me too," said Mrs. Kaye.

And so another day ended for the Kaye family.

In the morning, Benjamin awoke earlier than usual and found his mother in the kitchen, just beginning to prepare breakfast for the family.

"Good morning, Benjamin. Did you sleep well?"

"Morning, Mom. I slept okay, but I've been awake for the last hour wondering where we went wrong. I can't figure it out."

"Went wrong with what?"

"Where we dug. You know, for the treasure." He helped his mother set the table and pour juice.

"Maybe you just didn't dig deep enough," Mrs. Kaye suggested.

"Maybe, but I don't think that's it. We went pretty deep. We've got to be in the wrong place but I can't see how. The signs were so clear."

"I'm sure you and Martin will figure it out. Please call your father and brother to breakfast."

"Okay, Mom." Benjamin turned and yelled "**DAD**" directly into Mr. Kaye's armpit. "Oh, sorry, Dad, didn't see you there."

"Next time your mother says to call me, she means to come find me."

"Gotcha, Dad."

"**MAR**... I mean, I'll go wake Martin up and tell him to come to breakfast."

"Don't bother, I'm up," said Martin as he rubbed the sleep from his eyes. "Do you want to dig some more today, Benjamin?"

"Yeah, I do. But we've got to find a different spot. We've already dug halfway to China. We must be in the wrong place."

"I thought we were right about those signs," said Martin as he dug into his breakfast.

"I thought so, too," Benjamin replied. "But we must be reading them wrong."

"I don't see how. Everything points to where we're digging. You dig where you want, I'm staying in the same spot."

"Suit yourself. Hope you like Chinese food."

"Boys, what type of tree are you using for a marker?" asked Mrs. Kaye.

Martin responded. "It's a Native American tree."

"She means is it an oak tree or pine tree or like that, Martin."

"Oh, I don't know. Do you, Benjamin?"

"No. Why?"

"If you knew what kind of a tree it was, it might provide a clue for you."

"How's that?" Benjamin asked.

"Well, boys, you're digging based on how tall the tree is now," said Mrs. Kaye. "It wasn't always that tall."

"That's right!" said Benjamin. "Back when Bowlegs buried his treasure, Nat must have been much shorter."

"So how do we figure out how much it has grown since Billy was here?" wondered Martin.

"Good question, Martin. How do we, Mom?"

"What if you boys collect bark and leaf samples from the tree. At the library, we should be able to find a reference book to help us identify its genus and…"

"We don't need to know how smart the tree is Mom, we just…"

"She said *genus*, genius," said Benjamin.

"What? Wait – what?" said Martin.

"The genus and species can tell us how fast it grows. Right, Mom?"

"Exactly, Benjamin. And if we know the circumference, we can estimate Nat's age."

"I get it," said Martin. "What's a circumference?"

"It's a measurement of how big around something is," she replied.

"So you mean like Dad's belt measures his circumference?" asked Martin, smiling.

"Something like that, yes," answered Mrs. Kaye, giving her husband's tummy a friendly pat.

"How are we going to measure the circumference?" asked Benjamin.

No one was surprised when Mrs. Kaye produced a tape measure from one of her bags.

"Mom, you are amazing."

"Thank you, Benjamin. I do try to be prepared for anything."

Then, Benjamin groaned, "I can't believe it."

"What's that?"

"I can't believe Martin and I are asking to go to the library when we're on vacation at the beach. It's like you tricked us into making this an educational trip."

"Well, do you want to go to the library or not?" asked Mrs. Kaye.

"I do," said Martin.

"So do I," added Benjamin. "When can we go?"

"How about after our beach time. We'll go into town and have some lunch and then find the library."

"Sounds good to me," said Mr. Kaye. He had been listening to the discussion before bringing up a surprise he was planning for the boys. "And after the library, what do you boys say about going parasailing?"

"Really, Dad? Can we?" said Martin.

"Yes. Your mother and I have looked into it. We're convinced it is a safe activity run by a reputable company"

"Alright!" said Benjamin. He was the one who had asked his parents if they could parasail. Now that it was going to happen, he privately wondered if he would be too scared to go through with it. But, he didn't want anyone to know he was worried, especially Martin.

For the moment, he put his worries behind him as he and his family finished breakfast and cleaned up. That quickly done, they gathered their respective beach necessities and headed down to the beach. The boys brought the tape measure and a small plastic bag to hold the samples from Nat. As soon as they got to the beach and dropped their towels and other beach gear, the boys headed straight for the tree. A few minutes later they returned.

"Is this good enough, Mom?" asked Martin, showing her the bark and leaf samples from the tree.

"I think so. Looks like you two got very good samples for your research. We should have no problem identifying that Nat of yours."

The Kayes enjoyed their beach time and after several hours, returned to the condo, dressed, and left for town. They had a bite to eat at a little café that served excellent fish sandwiches. The library was just off the town square and down a block from a Native American Museum that looked interesting. Soon they were pouring over books about trees indigenous to northern Florida.

"The bark looks to be from a member of the oak family, don't you think?" said Mr. Kaye.

"I believe you're right," said Mrs. Kaye. "And, judging from the leaf, I would say we've identified a Quercus Laurifolia."

"A what?" asked Martin.

"That's the genus and species name for a tree that is more commonly know as the 'Diamond Oak,'" explained Mrs. Kaye.

"Sounds like a tree Billy Bowlegs would use to mark his treasure," said Martin.

"Does it say how fast it grows, Mom?" asked Benjamin.

"Let's see. Based on the growth patterns and how old it appears to be, I would estimate Nat to be about ten feet high when Billy came to this coast."

"That's great, Mom. I think you've earned a share of the treasure when we find it. Don't you, Martin?"

"I guess so. But we've done all the hard work, digging and stuff. We deserve the most."

"We might not have found it at all if it wasn't for Mom's idea," argued Benjamin.

"We still haven't found anything, Benjamin. Don't count your chickens before they cross the road," said Martin.

"What?"

"It's a saying."

"If you say so," said Benjamin, rolling his eyes.

"Do you boys still want to parasail?" asked Mr. Kaye.

"Yes," they answered in unison.

"Then let's go," said Mr. Kaye.

On the way, Martin had some questions.

"How high up will we be?"

"High enough, I expect," answered Mr. Kaye. "But we can sure ask them when we get there."

"Are you worried about it, Benjamin?" asked Martin.

"Well, to tell you the truth, I was. But now I'm looking forward to it. How 'bout you?"

"Well, I wasn't before. But now I'm kinda wondering if it's safe."

"Martin, we wouldn't let you do this if it wasn't safe," said Mrs. Kaye.

"Yeah, Martin, it'll be alright," said Benjamin.

They arrived ten minutes before their reserved time. That allowed them time to pay and to pick out life preservers. Soon, all four of them boarded the boat. Benjamin and Martin were hooked up to the parachute, and the boat left the shallows, heading out to the deeper water. As they picked up speed, the chute was let out. The boys, standing in their harnesses at the back of the boat, were lifted off their feet and gracefully rode the wind, climbing into the air until the line attached to them was fully extended.

Looking up from the boat, Mr. and Mrs. Kaye could not make out the expressions on the boys' faces. They hoped they were having fun and weren't too scared.

"It's like flying a human kite, isn't it?" said Mr. Kaye

"Yes. I hope the string doesn't break," replied Mrs. Kaye. "I wonder how it is up there?"

"Whoa, do you think we're going too high, Benjamin?" Martin was harnessed just below Benjamin and as their altitude rose higher and higher, so did his anxiety.

"It'll be okay, Martin. Just relax and enjoy the ride. Look, you can see our condo over there."

"Hey, you can. There's the pool. And I can see the place where we're digging. There's Nat."

"Looks pretty small from way up here."

"Everything is small from up here," said Martin. "I wonder what would happen if this rope broke?" he said.

"I guess we'd just float down to the water like we were parachuting. Then we'd swim to shore. It's not going to happen, but even if it did, it wouldn't be so bad. You could swim that easily. Especially with a life jacket," said Benjamin.

"That sounds like fun, sort of," said Martin.

After awhile, the crew began reeling the boys in. When they were near the boat, the pilot slowed down until the two boys' legs dipped into the water. The boat then sped up, sending them rapidly up into the air again. The last length of rope was reeled in and Martin and Benjamin landed softly on the back of the boat.

"That was fun," said Martin as he gained his footing. "I didn't know they were going to dunk us."

"That was our idea," said Mrs. Kaye. "We thought it would be a nice touch."

As they rode back to shore, the boys described the whole experience. They thanked their parents for letting them parasail and were proud of themselves for doing something brave.

"I wonder if Tip and Tap would have been afraid to parasail," asked Martin.

"I wonder," replied Mr. Kaye.

As soon as they got back to the condo, Benjamin and Martin hurried down to the beach to resume their search for treasure. They chose a new spot to dig based on their research. Their confidence was high, as was their excitement. But after another hard dig, they came up empty again.

"I just knew we were going to find it this time, Benjamin. I guess we were just wrong about this place all together."

"Yeah," said Benjamin. "We were stupid to think we could discover pirate treasure. Let's not waste any more time trying to find something that just isn't here."

"You're right. Let's go for a swim," said Martin.

"Good idea. Let's go."

Mr. and Mrs. Kaye were sitting under their umbrella, reading their books. Mrs. Kaye was pouring some lemonade for herself and Mr. Kaye as the boys arrived. She could see the disappointed looks on their faces.

"No luck, boys?"

"No," they both replied. Benjamin added, "It was dumb to waste our time with all that digging. We're never going to find anything."

Mr. Kaye spoke up after a long, thirst-quenching drink. "Boys, it seems to me it wasn't a waste of time. You were excited about the prospect of treasure. You used sound reasoning and even did some research so you could figure where to dig. You tried and you had fun in the process. Seems like a successful experience to me."

"If you say so, Dad," answered Benjamin. "But from now on, I think we'll leave the treasure hunting to Tip and Tap."

"Are you boys thirsty?" asked Mrs. Kaye. "I've got some lemonade all made up."

"Great," said Martin. "Thanks."

"Yeah, Mom, thanks," added Benjamin.

After they finished their drinks, Benjamin and Martin ran into the water for a swim. They swam while their parents watched from their beach chairs. When it was time, they all went up to the condo to get ready for dinner.

Mrs. Kaye liked to ask anyone she met at the beach about their favorite restaurants. She had developed such a long list they would never have time to try them all.

"We'd have to eat three dinners a day to make it to all these restaurants," Martin observed. He wished he could. He liked to eat.

The place they selected was just right for everyone, and they all enjoyed their dinner. Afterwards, back at the condo, the boys had their usual after dinner swim. Mr. and Mrs.

Kaye watched from lounge chairs, enjoying the pleasant evening and the laughter and play of their children.

Throughout the day and during dinner, the boys continued to express their concerns about Tip and Tap and all the trouble they had gotten themselves into. So, when Mr. and Mrs. Kaye said it was time to go up and get ready for bed, they immediately jumped out of the pool and ran up to their condo to get ready in a hurry.

An Audience with the Captain

Tip and Tap were taken to the *Tell No Tales* by Smelly John, Ears McGinty, and Mr. Gruntee. Although they weren't treated like honored guests, Mr. Smelling and Mr. McGinty were not too rough with them. They were, after all, just boys. But Mr. Gruntee had a personal bone to pick with the youngsters for getting him in so much trouble. On the way to the ship, he gave the boys several hard shoves.

"There's no need in that, Mr. Gruntee," said Smelly John, after a particularly hard push. "I expect they're in fer worse when they answer to the Captain."

"Well, it was their sneakin and thievin what got'em into this mess. And got me in mine with the Cap'n, too. They deserve what they get, and worse, if yer askin me."

"I'm not, far as I can tell. So just shut yer yap and keep yer hands off'n the lads unless they cause trouble," said Mr. Smelling. "And yer not plannin on causin any trouble, now are ya me lads?" asked Smelly John with a threatening sneer.

The boys were silent. They were frightened, certainly. But they had been in enough tight spots to know they had to keep their wits about them. These men were bigger, but Tip and Tap knew they could be outsmarted. They would have to wait for the right chance. And they would have to hope it would arise before things went too far. After all, Billy Bowlegs was not known for his charity or forgiveness. Neither of them said a thing to the pirates. They just listened carefully and tried to think of a way out of this mess.

Tip and Tap were taken below decks to the main hold of the ship. It was dark down there except for the light given off by the oil lamp Smelly John carried. Two pillars supporting the floor above stood about ten feet apart. Mr. Gruntee grabbed an old rope from a corner of the hold and tied a boy to each of the posts. Using the thick cord, he encircled their small bodies several times before tying it off with a hard pull.

"That ought'a hold'em. Hope you lads are comfortable," Mr. Gruntee said.

The men then left the hold and Tip and Tap were alone in the dark, wondering what would happen next and what they could do to make whatever did happen, go their way. "Are you alright, Tap? That Mr. Gruntee didn't hurt you, did he?"

"No, I'm okay. How 'bout you?"

"I'm fine. I'm just sorry I got you into this. I never figured on getting caught by this bunch."

"Don't blame yourself, Tip. I went along with it, knowing the risk," responded Tap. He added, "What do think Bowlegs'll do to us?"

"I'm afraid to think what he'll do. But there's a reason he didn't just kill us back on the island. He wants his diamonds back."

"But he must have all the treasure he could ever need. What's one diamond necklace to him?"

"I don't know, Tap, unless he just doesn't like to lose at anything. But if it's the necklace he wants, then it's the necklace he'll never get."

"Why not?"

"Cause the necklace is the only thing keepin us alive," said Tip.

Soon the boys heard heavy footsteps coming toward them. Tip tried not to let his brother see how scared he was. Tap was scared enough already.

Smelly John came in, carrying the same lamp. Captain Bowlegs followed him.

"Put the lamp down just there," the Captain directed. Mr. Smelling placed the lamp on the floor. "You may leave us now, Mr. Smelling. I'd like a word with the lads meself."

Smelly John left the room. Tip and Tap were alone with Captain Bowlegs. He stood just behind the lamp, which cast an awful glow on his face, making him look all the more scary and making a giant shadow of him play on the back wall and ceiling of the hold.

"You mean," interrupted Martin, "like when we camp out in the back yard and we put our flashlights up under our chins to make a scary face, Dad?"

"Why yes, Martin. I suppose that is how it looked."

"Cool," said Martin.

Mrs. Kaye quietly wondered if Martin needed to break the tension by asking questions once in a while. So did Benjamin, and this time he was patient with his brother's interruption.

"Shall I continue, then?" asked Mr. Kaye.

"Yes, please," responded Martin. "We have to get through the story so Tip and Tap can escape. They will escape, won't they, Dad?"

"I certainly hope so," said Mr. Kaye. "Are we ready to get on with the story?" he asked again.

"Yeah, this is good stuff," answered Benjamin.

"Yeah Dad, only, well, do you *think* they'll escape?"

"They're clever lads, to be sure, Martin," said Mr. Kaye, "but you never know with pirates. They can be a desperate lot."

111

"What do you think, Mom? Do you think Tip and Tap will get out of there?" Martin was having a hard time thinking about Tip and Tap being in the hands of pirates. He wanted them out of there as soon as possible.

"Martin, I think they'll be okay. So let's allow your father to continue. They won't get away if we don't continue the story."

"Good idea, Mom. Okay, Dad, fire away," said Martin.

☠

At first, Billy just stood, not saying a word. Then, he pulled up a crate and sat down facing them. When he finally spoke, it was in a hushed, angry tone.

"I want what's mine."

The boys said nothing. After a few moments, Bowlegs spoke again.

"I want what's mine," he repeated.

Still the boys were silent.

"Yer trying me patience, lads." He said this part quietly. "Few men, much less boys, have tried me patience and had anything good to say about the outcome. Now you boys took something that was mine." A bit louder he added, "I want it back. And yer gonna tell me where it is. If ya do, I might go easy on ya." Louder still, he said, "If not, you'll never be heard from again around these parts." He continued, almost shouting, "or any other parts fer that matter. Cause I'll be feedin yer parts to the sharks," he screamed.

Tip responded, as calmly as he could. "And what is it you think we have of yours, Captain Bowlegs?"

"Ah, the lad can speak, can he? That's good. Cause a'fore I'm done, you'll be singin from the yardarms anything I care to hear. Now where is it?"

"Where is what, Captain?" asked Tip.

"Ya know perfectly well what I'm talkin about. Me

necklace. That's what. I want to know where me necklace is."

"Which necklace is that, Captain?" asked Tip innocently. He knew he was pushing his luck, but he didn't know what else to do but see if he could gain more time to think.

"The diamond necklace. The one ya took from me cabin the night we landed here. Mr. Gruntee fell asleep on his watch and ended up pushed overboard fer his troubles. Can't say he didn't deserve it, the no good slouch of a watchman. Ya pushed him over and in the commotion, made yer escape."

"What makes you think it was us?" asked Tap. He had been quietly watching and decided to join in the conversation. He was scared, but he thought he'd take the heat off Tip for a moment.

"Cause you two are the only ones who have been payin such close attention to our doings around here. We saw ya in the woods the next day and should'a captured ya then. But ya outsmarted me men. Don't pat yerselves on the back fer that, though. It ain't hard to outsmart a bunch'a oafs like I've got with me. Then yer snooping around on Mystery Ally like maybe I'll just bury me treasure while yer watching so's you can help yerselves to it after I'm gone. No, don't play dumb with me. I know it was you two what took it and I know it's you two what's gonna return it."

"Whatever," said Tip.

Billy raised a hand to slap Tip but stopped himself. "Don't be gettin insolent with me, lad. You don't want to see me mad. I'll ask ya one more time. Where is it?"

"I don't know what you're talking about Captain Bowlegs," said Tip. "But if I run across a diamond necklace, I'll sure let you know."

Bowlegs was furious, but he decided not to push any harder just then. Calmly, he said, "Maybe you boys'll change yer story after you've had some time to think on it. I'll be back tomorrow, and ya better be ready to talk. If not, I could always let Mr. Gruntee have at ya. He's been wantin' to teach ya some manners, what with yer stealin on his watch and pushin'em overboard and all. Ya made him look right foolish, ya did. I suspect it would be a long, tough lesson he'd like to teach. In the meantime, you'll not be gettin food nor drink from any o'me crew. Hope you boys are comfortable. It figures to be a long night."

Billy picked up the lamp and left. After waiting a long time to be sure they were alone, the boys began to speak about the fix they were in.

"We've got to get out of here, Tap. These pirates are gonna lose patience and then there's no telling what they'll do to us."

"I know," said Tap, "but how?"

"If I could reach into my pocket, I've got a shell in there. I'll bet if I broke it, the edge would be sharp enough to cut through these ropes." As usual, the boys were just wearing shorts. No shirts, no shoes. The problem with reaching into his pocket was Tip's arms were pinned to his sides. He couldn't lift them up high enough along his body to reach his pocket. He could feel the shell with his right thumb, through the fabric of his shorts. He explained this to Tap, who thought it very bad luck his brother was tied in such a way as to prevent him from being able to use the one object that might help them get loose. And even if they were to get loose, how would they ever get off the ship before they were discovered? They couldn't give up hope yet, though. There had to be a way to get to that shell.

All at once, Tap had an idea. "Tip, can you break the shell while it's still in your pocket?"

"Maybe, but why?" asked Tip.

"If you can get a sharp enough edge on the shell, maybe you could make it cut through your pocket. That way, you could get at it without having to reach into the pocket."

"Good idea, Tap. But even if I can, it'll take awhile."

"Well, like Billy said, it figures to be a long night. Let's hope we have enough time to get loose and get out of here before they come back for us."

Tip was able to pinch the shell using his thumb and index finger. He worked it around until he had it the way he wanted it. Then, after several failed attempts, he managed to snap it in two. Left now were two half shells, both of which felt like they had sharp edges.

"First stage accomplished," he told Tap who watched nervously. "Now let's see if I can poke a hole through these shorts."

That proved to be harder than he thought. But after diligently working at it for what seemed like hours, Tip succeeded in poking a hole through his pocket and could feel the edge of the shell.

"I've got it, Tap. Now all I have to do is cut through this rope."

Just then, they heard a voice coming from behind the door to the hold. It froze them in fear.

Martin moved a little closer to his father. As he did so, Mr. Kaye seemed to be quoting one of the pirates.

"A shame, that's what 'tis."

The door opened. It was Ears McGinty. He had been listening behind the door. Tip and Tap felt their hopes plunge into despair. Surely, this was it for them. There was no way to escape if they couldn't cut through the ropes that held them.

"Aha. I thought me ears picked up on talk of cuttin rope. Very clever of ya to have gotten hold of a broken shell," he snickered. "Moost'a picked it up when Mr. Farsythe knocked ya down. No matter. I'll joost be relievin ya of it now, that's a good lad. Boys shouldn't be playing with sharp objects."

Tip opened his hand and McGinty took the shell fragment.

McGinty continued, "Wouldn't want ya getting hurt. At least not till we have a chance to hurt ya." His laugh had no humor. "Now you behave yerselves like good lit'le lads and try to get some sleep. You'll be needin yer wits about ya come mornin. That's when the Captain aims to deal with ya, first thing come sun up."

McGinty left and closed the door behind him.

When he left, Tap said, "He's got the biggest ears I've ever seen."

"I heard that," said Ears from behind the door.

"Yeah," replied Tip. "They work pretty well, too."

"Heard that, too," McGinty added.

"I guess he's right," said Tip. "We better just rest, best we can. There's no way to get away now. That broken shell was our last hope."

"But Tip," Tap started to whisper, "you've still..."

Just then, Ears called in, "Stop yer yammerin now or I'll be in there again."

"Alright," yelled Tip. "Quiet now, Tap. We don't want to disturb that fella anymore."

Tip wanted the pirate to believe he was angry and frustrated his plan had been discovered. And he didn't want Tap to say what he was about to say. While he was answering Mr. McGinty, he had already begun to work the other shell half out of his pocket.

Tap could just make out what his brother was doing. He knew they couldn't talk about escape with that big-eared lout listening. So he thought for a minute, and then said quietly, "I guess there's nothing we can do now. Let's try

116

to get some rest and maybe things will look up for us in the morning."

"I hope you're right," replied Tip.

"I wouldn't count on it," came the final word from Mr. McGinty.

After that, the boys were quiet for a long time. Tip knew his brother had caught on to what he was doing and had acted hopeless to throw McGinty off. He had been working diligently all the while, to cut through one of the cords of rope that bound him. It was slow work and several times he almost lost his grip on the shell. His palm was cut, and several of his fingers as well, from his efforts. Tap couldn't see Tip's hand, but he heard a drop of something hit the deck now and then, and figured his brother was having to endure a fair amount of pain. He knew Tip wouldn't stop just because of a little blood, though.

It seemed as if the night would never end. At the same time, morning, and whatever would come with it, loomed ever closer at hand. The boys had no idea what time it was, but knew they had to be free by sun up. Not being able to talk made the time go even slower. Eventually, Tap nodded off.

When it seemed he must be running out of time, not to mention strength and hope, Tip felt the rope give way. When it did, it loosened the cords wrapped around him so he could, after a great deal of wriggling and twisting, manage to get one arm loose. He then made short order of getting free. Tip carefully laid the rope down, not making a sound. He immediately went to Tap, who was asleep. He covered Tap's mouth as he gently woke him so Tap's surprise didn't give them away. Tap was thrilled to see his brother had gotten free. He waited silently as Tip worked to untie him.

Aided by thin strands of light just beginning to seep into their chamber and announcing the arrival of morning and whatever might come with it, the boys began to assess their surroundings. The room was filled with barrels and crates stacked high atop one another. The only door the boys could find was the one the big-eared pirate had gone through. There had to be another way out. They examined the floor, looking for hatches or openings but found none. Then they looked to the ceiling high above them. There was a large set of doors that must have allowed cargo to be lowered through from above. They looked heavy, but if they could be pried open somehow, maybe that would be the escape route the boys needed. Tip and Tap climbed toward the ceiling, being careful not to jostle the crates and barrels or make any sound that could give them away. Tap reached the doors first, but couldn't budge them. Tip climbed up to help, but the door was too heavy even for the two of them working together. Maddening as it was, the boys realized they could not escape by that route. They were feeling more hopeless and frightened by the minute.

Tip motioned for Tap to follow him as he climbed toward one end of the room. He thought if the pirates came in and found them missing, they might assume the boys had already escaped. They found a crate against the corner of the room, about half way to the ceiling. They sat down, feeling their luck was running out. But as Tap leaned against the wall, it gave way and he fell backward into a small chamber. There had been no sign of a door there. Tip quickly followed his brother and swung the door closed.

They were now in a small, long room, not more than a wide hallway, really. And in that small room was more treasure than the boys ever dreamed existed in all the world.

They stood, mesmerized by the sight in front of them. Everywhere they looked, they could see treasure. If gold and silver coins weren't spilling out of open chests, diamonds, emeralds, and rubies were. On one side of the wall sat statues of solid gold. It was all of the stories of Captain Billy Bowlegs' fabulous treasure and ten times that. It was what they had been hoping for, ever since they watched Billy sail into the waters of the Emerald Coast. They had found Bowlegs' bounty and it terrified them. If Bowlegs knew they had discovered his hiding place, he would surely see them dead.

While Tap continued to look at the horde of riches, Tip's mind turned back to matters at hand. They still had to find a way out. Tip reasoned the captain would not want his treasure too far from him. If that were true, then perhaps Billy's cabin lay at the other end of the passage. Going to the far wall, he discovered a small door leading to another chamber. A small space allowed Tip and then Tap also, to peer through. Tip had guessed correctly. His sword at his side and his handgun and dagger in his belt, Billy looked as if he were preparing for battle. Then they heard him speak.

"I'll get it back. All these years I've missed ya. But I've always had yer picture and the necklace to remind me of ya – to make me feel you were still with me in a way."

He was talking to a picture the boys could see clearly. It was an old picture of a young woman who seemed to gaze out of the gold frame as if she was looking at the one she loved most in all the world. And she was wearing the necklace.

"Hard, it was, when we lost Father. And harder still, a year later, when yer death made me an orphan. I was lost. When I could no longer have me family, I vowed then and there to always have whatever else I wanted. To take it if I had to, or die tryin. I've robbed, murdered, and cheated me way to a king's ransom and then some. But none of it really matters as much as the necklace Father gave ya on yer weddin day. The necklace what was handed down to him by his father. A reminder of better times it was . . ."

Billy paused. He appeared to be remembering things far off in the past. Then he continued. "And I'll get it back so's I can have that small piece of ya and the last love I ever felt in me life. I'll retrieve it or them's what took it will know me full wrath."

The boys crouched silently, just a few feet from Billy and his fury. They knew he would leave soon to go question them. When he did, they planned to enter his cabin and make their way to the upper deck somehow. As they waited, Tip tried to remember everything he could about the layout of the ship. He could picture the crew's quarters where he heard Mr. Gruntee snoring the night he stole the necklace. He thought he remembered seeing other doors along the hall and the Captain's cabin at one end. If they were lucky, maybe they could escape during the confusion when they were discovered missing.

Captain Bowlegs was finally ready. He opened the door to the hallway and left his cabin. The boys knew they had to act quickly. Taking one last look at the treasure they were leaving behind, Tip and Tap pushed through the door. From the inside, they could see the doorway was completely concealed. It looked just like part of the wall.

"Must be a passage only Billy knows about," whispered Tip.

"I wonder if all the stories of buried treasure are just that, stories. Looks like Ol'Billy likes to keep his treasure close to home," said Tap.

Suddenly, they heard a blood-curdling scream from below. Their escape had been discovered. The boys quickly stepped back into the cabin as several doors opened and men came running down the hall.

"They must be going down below to help look for us, Tap. If they're going down, we'll go up."

As soon as it was quiet, they opened the door and bolted to the steps leading up to the main deck. It wasn't hard to imagine what was happening below decks.

The boys figured to get to the main deck, jump overboard, and swim to their freedom. But when they got up on deck, they knew they were in trouble. As they made their way to the port side, they heard men below, then saw them climbing up over the railing. They sprinted toward the starboard side and almost ran into a gang of men just reaching the deck. There was nowhere to turn. They were surrounded.

The crew, assuming they were under attack when they heard Bowlegs' roar, had mustered to man the cannons. Billy quickly realized the prisoners would make for the main deck so he ordered his men to crawl through the gunnery positions and get to the upper deck before the boys could jump over. The crew had had more than enough of these pesky brats and, with blood in their eyes, closed in on the boys.

It looked to be a hard end for the boys after they had worked so hard to escape. As the crew advanced, the only direction Tip and Tap had to go was up. Jumping and reaching for the rigging of the main sail, they began to climb toward the crow's nest. The boys were quick and they put some distance between the angry marauders and themselves. But the first pirate to reach the rigging closed the gap in a hurry. When the boys looked down, they could see the gleam of his dagger between his teeth as it reflected the rays of the sun.

"Scully'll catch'em," Captain Bowlegs said to Mr. Smelling. "He's the quickest we've got. But just in case, send up a few more men. We'll take nothin fer granted with these escape artists."

"Aye, aye, sir. Mr. Farsythe, see'n as how they're headin fer yer perch, up ya go after'em. And take McGinty and Gruntee with ya."

"It'll be me pleasure, Mr. Smelling. Let's go men."

Each of the men climbing into the rigging had a personal bone to pick with Tip and Tap and couldn't wait to get their hands on them. Tap had almost reached the crow's nest and Tip was right behind him. He made sure he stayed between the advancing pirate and his younger brother. Scully was close enough to strike and, drawing his dagger,

121

made a mad lunge at Tip's head. To avoid the blow, he swung out over the sail, hanging on to its edge. The dagger just missed Tip and sliced through a part of the sail like a hot knife cutting through butter.

"Tap, this way," yelled Tip. He wanted his brother to follow him along the edge of the sail and away from the angry pirate. But with the two boys hanging on to the sail, the rip began to get bigger. Soon, the boys could feel themselves being slowly lowered toward the deck as the sail they clung to ripped more and more. They tried desperately to keep climbing but it was like going up a down escalator. They were sinking fast.

"Dad, I don't think they had escalators back then," Benjamin pointed out. The family had listened attentively for about as long as they could, and someone had to break the tension.

"Well, you're right, Benjamin. I'm just trying to help you picture what was happening."

"It does, Dad," said Martin. "Now let's get back to the story. We can't just leave Tip and Tap hanging like that."

"Right, everybody ready to resume the story?" asked Mr. Kaye.

"Absolutely," said Martin.

"Yes," said Mrs. Kaye.

"Fire away, Dad," replied Benjamin.

The rigging had caught on Tip's feet and the torn sail was getting bunched up below him.

"Keep climbing, Tap. We've got to stay aloft or we're captured for sure."

"I'm trying," shouted Tap.

The boys pulled themselves up, but each time they did, the sail ripped even more, resulting in a temporary stalemate between the boys' efforts to stay aloft and gravity's efforts to bring them down. Finally, the rip in the sail was complete. The pirates on deck and those up in the rigging cheered as the boys slowly slipped to their doom.

Then, just as they were about to be delivered to the waiting mob below, a strong gust of wind caught the sail from below and lifted the boys up and away from Billy and his crew. The pirates' cheers turned to angry and incredulous shouts of dismay as the boys were snatched from their grasp.

"Hang on," shouted Tip as the boys were lifted high in the air and clear of the ship. The sail, acting like a parachute, caught the now steady air current that was blowing toward the shore. The boys clung to the rigging as they floated away from the ship and the stunned men below.

A Visit to History

That was great. I knew Tip and Tap would get away. I just couldn't figure out how. But they did. They got away. They flew away from those old pirates and left them in their dust. They smoked 'em. Those pirates never knew what hit 'em. Don't come messing with Tip and Tap unless you bring all you got, Captain Bowlegs, cause you da man, Tip! You da man, Tap! Yes!"

"So, you liked the story, Martin?" asked Mr. Kaye.

"Oh, yeah. That was the best. I gotta tell you, though, I was getting a little nervous."

"Gee, I couldn't tell. I thought you always bit your toenails," said Benjamin.

"Yeah, well you can bite my…"

"Martin! That's more than enough of that."

"Sorry, Mom."

"And you, Benjamin?" asked Mr. Kaye.

"What?"

"How did you like the story?"

"I thought it was great, too. Good job, Dad."

"Thank you. Now apologize to your brother."

"Sorry, Martin."

"That's okay. I'm just glad Tip and Tap are finally safe."

"Oh, I wouldn't say they're safe, exactly," said Mr. Kaye.

"What do you mean, Dad?" asked Benjamin.

"Well, son, Tip and Tap are being blown through the air toward shore, but they're a long way from being safe."

"They'll be okay. It's just like Martin and me this afternoon. They'll dip into the water nice and gentle like. Then they'll swim to shore. Bowlegs is still out to sea. They escaped. They're golden now."

Mr. Kaye made the boys nervous when he replied, "We'll see."

"Off you go to sleep, now," said Mrs. Kaye. She gave both boys a hug and kiss and tucked them in. Mr. Kaye followed behind and collected his goodnight hugs and kisses, too. "Good night, boys," he said. "Sleep tight."

"Good night, Dad," they answered. "See you in the morning," added Benjamin.

"Yeah, in the morning, Dad," responded Martin.

Mr. and Mrs. Kaye turned out the lights and left the boys to their sleep and dreams of floating through the sky and of overflowing treasures.

"Good story, hon," said Mrs. Kaye. "But I must disagree with part of Martin's assessment."

"Which part?"

"About Tip and Tap. Cause I think you da man. You are definitely da man."

Morning brought Thursday with it, the second to last day the Kayes would have on the Emerald Coast. Vacation time was becoming a precious commodity and no one wanted to waste a minute of it. The boys abandoned their search for Bowlegs' treasure. As Benjamin had pointed out to Martin, "We've figured everything right, and there's just nothing there. No sense wasting our time digging holes when we could be swimming in the ocean." That logic was hard for an eight year old from the midwest to argue with, especially on the next to last day he would be near the ocean for maybe the whole entire rest of his life.

After lunch, they planned to visit the museum they had noticed near the library. They thought it would be a good way to explore more about the history of their vacation spot. After spending time at the museum, they would return to the beach for the afternoon and early evening.

The boys played hard at the beach. In the high waves, they worked to perfect their body surfing technique. Try as he might, Martin couldn't quite compete with his older brother. Benjamin always seemed able to catch the waves just right and ride them almost to shore. Martin was good at catching waves too, but he had to concede Benjamin was the champion body surfer, at least between the two of them.

When it was close to noon, they left the beach and returned to the condo. While their parents prepared lunch, the boys showered and dressed to go to the museum.

"Can you believe we're leaving the beach a second day in a row to go do something educational?" asked Benjamin.

"I know," said Martin. "And I'll bet Mom and Dad are loving it."

"Yeah, but the funny thing is, I'm looking forward to it, as well," admitted Benjamin.

"Me too," said Martin.

After lunch, the Kayes drove the few miles to the museum. They were immediately struck by the sense of going back in time as they browsed among ancient examples of Native American tools and other items dating back thousands of years. The museum housed an impressive collection of prehistoric ceramics from the area, many of which were excavated from the Temple Mound around which the museum was built. They learned archeologists and museum curators from the Smithsonian Institute had studied the mound and its contents over 100 years earlier.

"This stuff is really old," observed Martin.

"Gee, ya think?" responded Benjamin.

"I mean, it's really cool Native Americans used this stuff so long ago."

Benjamin had to agree. "Yeah, it is. It's very cool," he said.

The boys were interested to learn about the Native American tribes that lived on the Emerald Coast so many years ago. They also found examples of objects left behind by early European settlers, civil war soldiers, and *local pirates*.

"Benjamin, look at this stuff. That's a belt buckle from a real pirate."

"Yeah, and check this out, Martin, a cannon ball fired from a real pirate ship."

"No way! That's awesome," exclaimed Martin. Then he and his brother spotted something at the same time.

"Whoa, look at that," said Martin.

Benjamin whistled his approval. "Pirate gold. Probably the only pirate gold on the whole coast now."

The gold coins were piled around a small chest. The chest was constructed of strips of wood that must have darkened significantly over the years with bands of metal, encircling the chest. The top was arched with a gold plate on the front. Engraved into the gold were the letters *TNT*. When the Kayes saw the inscription, a common chill ran down each of their spines.

"I don't believe it," whispered Martin. "Dad, does that mean what I think it means?" he asked.

"Martin, I'm as surprised as you are. I'm not sure what it means. I never knew what Billy's ship was named. I did read he was given credit for the saying, "Dead men tell no tales," and I thought calling the ship the *Tell No Tales* sounded rather ominous and pirate-like. But the *TNT* here must be a coincidence. It is rather uncanny, though."

"It certainly is that," agreed Mrs. Kaye. "Uncanny."

"Unreal," added Benjamin.

"It must be Billy's treasure. Who else would have a treasure chest that said it was from the *Tell No Tales*?" asked Martin. There was no convincing him of a coincidence or pointing out that Billy's ship might have had a different name. He was certain he was gazing upon the notorious Captain Bowlegs' treasure. "That must be worth a fortune," he added.

The curator of the museum came over to the family when he noticed their intense interest in the exhibit.

"Hello, my name is Fact, Artemus Fact. My friends call me Artie. And anyone who takes an interest in our local history is counted among my friends. How do you do?"

"Very well, thank you, Artie," said Mr. Kaye. "We were just wondering about your display here."

It was not unusual for the treasure to catch the eye of the museum's visitors. But after the Kayes explained their interest in the engraved gold plate, the museum director got an amused look on his face.

"I don't mean to be rude, but I do find this to be a funny coincidence," he said.

"What do you mean?" asked Mrs. Kaye.

"Well, we can't be certain who buried this treasure, but we do know Captain Billy Bowlegs came to these shores at least twice, about ten years apart. Local historians refer to this find as Bowlegs' Bounty."

"Is that a fact?" asked Mrs. Kaye.

"As a matter of fact, it is," said Mr. Fact. "Furthermore, although again we can't be certain, there are those of us who believe you are correct about what the *TNT* means. You might also be interested in learning this chest was found surrounded by the remains of a human skeleton.

So, perhaps someone discovered the man burying this treasure and paid for his curiosity with his life. After all, nothing could be more true than the saying, 'Dead men tell no tales.'"

As he uttered those words, the Kayes all stared at the chest. Mr. Kaye wondered if he had forgotten reading about the *Tell No Tales* and added it to the story as if he was making it up. Either way, it was an interesting twist and the Kayes were glad they had decided to visit the museum.

They thanked Mr. Fact for sharing this information with them and praised his fine museum.

"Well worth the time to come and learn more about the history of the area, wouldn't you say?" asked Mrs. Kaye as they all climbed into the car and headed back to the condo.

"I certainly would," agreed Mr. Kaye. "How about you boys? What did you think?"

"Definitely worth the trip," said Martin.

"Freaky," said Benjamin. "I am completely weirded out."

"I believe I agree with your assessment, if not your vocabulary," said Mrs. Kaye.

When they got back to the condo and prepared to head to the beach, it was late afternoon. Many people were packing up for the day. Soon the Kayes felt like they had the whole seashore to themselves. The surf had died down, and the boys enjoyed snorkeling and searching for sea creatures. They found a starfish and several hermit crabs, among other things. After showing their parents each find, they returned the critters to the sea. Mr. and Mrs. Kaye enjoyed sitting and watching their sons enjoying the water.

"They sure have taken to the ocean for two boys from the midwest, haven't they?" asked Mrs. Kaye.

"They have, indeed," agreed Mr. Kaye.

Just then, the boys came out of the water. They could tell it was getting close to dinnertime but wanted to know if they could stay down at the beach longer.

"Actually, boys, we are having dinner right here. Your father and I are going up to prepare a beach picnic for dinner."

"Alright!" said Martin. "And we can stay on the beach all night?"

"Well, we can stay here until bedtime if you'd like," answered Mr. Kaye.

"I like," answered Martin.

"Me too," added Benjamin.

"Well then, how about if you boys stay on the beach, but don't go in the water, and your father and I will go prepare our picnic," said Mrs. Kaye. "Are you ready, Mr. Kaye?"

"Quite," said Mr. Kaye. "Shall we?" He extended a crooked elbow toward his wife. She slid her arm through his, and they walked, arm and arm, back to the condo.

"I hope no one sees them walking like that," said Martin.

"I know what you mean," agreed Benjamin. "But they are kinda cute in their own weird way."

"Whatever," said Martin.

The picnic was a big success and the family loved having the beach virtually to themselves. They all agreed it was the most pleasant dinner and evening they had spent yet. They planned to do the same thing the next night, their last, before heading home the following morning.

As it grew dark, the boys finally came out of the water and Mr. and Mrs. Kaye wrapped each of them in big, soft beach towels. They sat as a family and talked quietly about their day. After awhile, talk turned to Tip and Tap and what might happen next. As usual, Mr. Kaye took a, "You'll have to wait and see," approach to the boys' questions. Realizing he would not give them a preview of the night's story, the boys decided the thing to do was to get ready for bed. So, the dinner items and utensils were gathered up, as were the beach towels and toys, and the family headed up to the condo to prepare for bed and for the continuing adventures of Tip and Tap.

The Chase is On

Tip and Tap barely had time to appreciate their good fortune when they realized they had other things to worry about. They knew they could not hope to stay aloft all the way to shore. As it turned out, they were still a long way out to sea when they finally came to a soft, wet landing. Tip had some trouble untangling his feet from the rigging of the ruined sail. But he had anticipated that problem while still aloft and was able to free himself just before he and Tap plunged into the water. Leaving the sail that had saved their lives behind, the boys began the arduous task of swimming the long distance to shore.

After they had been swimming for some time, Tap felt he needed a rest so he turned over to float on his back. Tip did the same but as he did, the boys saw the terrifying sight of the *Tell No Tales* bearing down on them.

"Billy'll wreck the ship for sure if he doesn't slow down." Tip shouted.

"I don't think he cares. Let's get out of here," yelled Tap.

Back on the *Tell No Tales*, Billy and his crew had stood, gaping open-mouthed at the boys' improbable escape – but not for long. Gathering his wits and setting aside his rage and frustration, Bowlegs commanded his crew to make speedy pursuit. The ship was brought about and headed directly for the beachhead the boys were working hard to reach. Captain Bowlegs planned to outrun the boys to shore, even if he risked the ruin of his ship in the shallows along the coast. If he failed to catch the boys in the water, he would pursue them on land with all his strength and that of his crew.

The boys didn't know if they could outrun the ship, but they sure didn't want to stay around to debate the issue. Redoubling their efforts, they swam faster, but it felt like they were swimming in place as the *Tell No Tales* gained on them every second. The boys had three things in their favor, though. The ship's mainsail was gone so she couldn't muster her top speed. They also were almost to shallows where the ship couldn't follow them. And, if they could reach the safety of land, they would have a good chance of losing the pirates in the woods.

Billy stood in the prow of the ship, hatred and malice in his eyes as his ship sped toward his prey. His mind was bent on recapturing the boys and making them pay for their thievery and audacity to think they could get the better of him. He was so intent on catching them he didn't notice the shallow water until it was too late to save the ship from damage. She was almost upon Tip and Tap when the ship came to an abrupt halt, throwing Billy and the other crewmembers forward and off their feet. As Billy regained his footing, he was already shouting orders to his crew.

"Man the dinghy, men. Have it in the water in record time or I'll have yer hides. I want every last man with me. I mean to catch those boys if it's the last unholy thing I do on this earth."

Mr. Smelling responded with the efficiency of someone born to the life of a sailor. In no time, the small boat was launched, overflowing with pirates mad with fury that these boys had caused so much trouble for everyone. Acting as one, they set out to pursue their goal. The only discord among the men at that point was who would have the honor of teaching those boys a lesson once they were apprehended. There was no shortage of volunteers.

Soon the boys were not swimming as much as they were jogging and clawing their way to the beach. Their lungs felt on fire and they knew the chase was just beginning. The beach, with its soft white sand that had always looked so friendly and inviting, now loomed ahead of them like a white band of dangerous quicksand, slowing down their strides and making them work twice as hard for each step they took.

As the boys reached the beach, the pirates were jumping out of the dinghy into the shallow water. Now they were doing the clawing and scrambling. And, most of them were just starting their strenuous efforts, having ridden on the ship and then in the dinghy this far. Even the men who manned the oars where not leg weary. The same could not be said for Tip and Tap. By the time they were crossing from the soft sand to the harder ground of the woods they were nearly spent. And their pursuers were closing fast.

Tip and Tap felt more secure once they gained the shelter of the woods, hoping their knowledge of the trails would allow them to escape easily. But the boys underestimated the strength of the hatred that pushed the pirates. The marauders ran as if possessed and in no time were in the woods with the boys, close enough to hear their angry grumbling and feel the reverberation from their footsteps.

We've got to shake these thugs or we'll lead them right to our home, thought Tip. He thought about splitting up and trying to draw them away from Tap. Maybe Tap could reach the safety of their house and he could double back after having lost the pirates for good. He was afraid to get separated from Tap, though. And what if half of the pirates went after Tap? Tip would have no way of knowing if his brother was safe or in the clutches of the angry mob.

Then Tip figured out where they had to go. As they ran, he motioned for Tap to follow him toward an inland lake, surrounded by rocky terrain the boys had discovered months ago. It was their best place when they were hiding for fun and it might now be their best chance of staying alive. Tap caught on to Tip's plan and nodded his approval. Ordinarily, he would have smiled at the thought of going to their hideout, but at this point, his face showed only a grim look of determination. He knew they had to make it to safety, or else.

Besides staying ahead of the pirates, who showed no evidence of slowing down or ending their pursuit, the boys had other problems to deal with. For one thing, they were hungry. They had not eaten since the previous morning. And, they were tired. Tap had managed a bit of fitful sleep while tied to the post. But Tip was forced to work through the night without a break. The boys' energy reserves were running out.

Unfortunately for the brothers, the pirates showed no signs of fatigue. Tip and Tap could hear a crowd of them not far behind. What the boys couldn't have known, was Billy had halted his chase, along with Mr. Farsythe, at the point where Tip had altered his course. Mr. Farsythe wondered why the Captain stopped him there, and he soon found out.

Billy had a studying sort of look on his face. "Mr. Farsythe, let's study on this."

"Aye, Cap'n," replied Mr. Farsythe, grateful for the chance to catch his breath.

"Did ya happen to notice the boys changed course here?"

"Aye, sir, now ya mention it, I believe they did. They

were on a straight heading and then took a hard turn to port."

"Exactly," replied Billy. "And I'm thinkin I know why. The boys are no strangers to these woods, that's clear. The night Mr. Smelling and Mr. McGinty were almost fed to that giant cat was evidence enough they know their way around these parts. We also know they're clever. No doubt they've a plan to lose us in the woods, and I believe their plan will work."

"Sounds like you've a plan of yer own, Cap'n."

"I believe the boys were unnerved by our close pursuit and, reacting with fear, made a fatal mistake."

"What mistake was that, Cap'n?"

Confidently, Billy explained his deductions.

"Now that's usin yer noggin, Cap'n."

"Thank you, Mr. Farsythe. Now then, follow the trail the men took. You'll probably find them somewhere along the path, scratchin their fool heads and wonderin how they could lose those two again. Bring the men back to me and after they go on about their latest blunders, we'll organize our next move."

Mr. Farsythe found the men just as the Captain predicted. They were standing on the edge of a rocky cliff, overlooking a pretty, secluded lake. Smelly John told of the chase, describing how they had seen the boys turn a corner of the trail not fifty steps ahead of them. When the pirates came to the same turn seconds later, the boys had disappeared. The only direction the boys could have gone was down, into the lake. But there was no way they could have crossed it without being seen. From that vantage point, the entire lake was visible. The pirates had waited and watched the lake closely. But, after waiting for some time, the band of pirates was confused and terribly frustrated. Somehow, they had lost the boys again, or more accurately, the boys had lost them.

"I guess we'll have t'make our excuses to the Cap'n again," said Smelly John, "although I can't say I'm looking forward to it."

"I wouldn't worry too much about that, John," said Mr. Farsythe. "He told me I'd likely find ya like this. But he's got the lads figured, this time. I'm to lead ya back to the Captain. Don't worry. We'll get those rascals yet, wherever they are."

Those same two young rascals weren't far. They had made it to the cliff just in time to dive into the lake far below without being seen. They knew to make their disappearance seem real, they had to be under the water before the pirates could spot them. The gang of pirates made so much noise as they pursued Tip and Tap, they didn't hear the splash as the boys plunged perfectly into the cool water.

The trail ended so abruptly the pirates in the lead almost fell over the cliff. In the confusion, no one noticed the small ripples emanating in circles from the boys' points of entry. The pirates had good reason to be scratching their heads in wonderment. The boys did seem to just vanish. The baffled gang would have been surprised to learn that Tip and Tap, at that moment, were sitting, drying off and resting, almost directly below them. They were in a cave they called their hideout. The boys were certain they were the only living souls who knew about it because the entrance to the cave was under water. The boys discovered it one day when they were having contests to see who could stay underwater the longest. Tap won the competition that day by staying under for over five minutes. He was able to do that by swimming up into the opening of the cave and finding fresh air. After he was sure he would win the contest, he plunged back into the water, under the rock, and back to the surface. Tip was about to dive in looking for him when Tap surfaced and told him of his discovery.

Since then, they had spent many leisurely hours swimming in the lake and disappearing into their hideout.

They never figured Tap's discovery would save their necks. They were very grateful they had decided to stock the cave with essential hideout supplies. There were candles, matches, and more importantly, some dried beef and hard candy. The boys had wrapped these items in oilcloth to keep them dry. They were glad to have a chance to rest and recuperate from the last two arduous days.

The beef jerky and candy provided welcome relief for their hunger.

"This is the best meal I've ever had," said Tap.

"I know what you mean," responded Tip. "I didn't realize how hungry I was, or how tired now that I think about it. I'm exhausted."

"Me too," said Tap."

"Let's let Bowlegs and his band cool their heels awhile. Maybe they'll get discouraged and head back to the ship. Meanwhile, I'm gonna get some shut eye."

"Sounds good to me," agreed Tap.

It didn't matter the sleeping surface wasn't quite as soft as their beds at home. The boys slept on, and like, rocks. After several hours, they weren't really certain how many, the boys awoke. During the daytime, the pool leading into the cave had a certain luminescence to it. The boys saw none now, so figured it was nighttime.

"Wait a minute, Dad."

"Yes, Martin, what is it?" asked Mr. Kaye.

"What does lumin-sence or whatever you said mean?"

"Luminescence," Mrs. Kaye corrected. "It means to glow."

"Oh. Why didn't you just say glow then, instead of a word no one ever heard of," wondered Martin.

"Because, dip wad, Dad is trying to teach us some new vocabulary words," said Benjamin.

"That's correct, Benjamin, except for the dip wad remark. That's not on the list of acceptable vocabulary words."

"Sorry, Dad. You're not a dip wad Martin, at least not most of the time."

"Gee thanks, Benjamin, neither are you, some of the time."

"Getting back to the story..."

☠

The boys figured it had been long enough for Billy to give up the search and return to the ship. Tip thought it would be best if he checked to make sure the coast was clear. If it was, he would swim back to get Tap. If he did not return, Tap was to stay in the cave for two days, then try to find help.

Plunging into the water, he swam down under the rock ledge and back up to the surface of the lake. It wasn't long before Tap saw him resurface.

"It looks clear up there. I think Billy must'a given up."

"I hope so," said Tap. "Let's go."

The boys dove together into the cool water and in no time were climbing out of the lake, listening for signs of danger. After they felt confident the pirates had gone, they carefully climbed the rocky cliff and made their way through the forest. It took longer than usual to get home due to the care they took to avoid any pirates or other dangerous creatures that might be lurking. They stayed off the regular trail, keeping to the dense forest areas. Every now and then, they would quietly creep toward the path to see if the pirates were still searching for them.

After an hour or so of this, though, the boys began to

feel more and more safe. In fact, by the time they arrived at the clearing and could see their house, they had all but forgotten about the close call with the pirates. Glad to be home, they were weary and hungry again and couldn't wait to fix themselves a good meal and sleep in their own beds.

"I bet I sleep till next week, once I hit that bed," said Tap.

"Me too," added Tip. "But I aim to be well fed when my head hits that pillow."

"Oh, yeah. Let me at the food," said Tap.

Tap opened the door to the cabin and the boys went in, relieved to be in the safety of their own home. As they found a match and lit a candle, relief turned to horror.

"Evenin, laddies. Nice of ya to drop by. 'Tis a shame we can't offer ya a bite to eat as we've just finished the last of the provisions."

It was, of course, Captain Billy Bowlegs himself, right in their house, sitting at their table, and eating their food. Tip and Tap turned to bolt for the door, but Mr. Gruntee, Mr. Farsythe, and Smelly John barred their way. The boys scanned the room to see the whole group of pirates surrounding them, taking liberties with their possessions and their home.

"Now then," continued Captain Bowlegs as he put his feet up on the table and pushed his chair back to a reclining position, "about me diamonds."

Friday Arrives Uninvited

"Ro way," said Benjamin. "Their goose is really cooked now."

"Dad, Billy and his pirates can't be in their house," said Martin. "You should change that part."

"Yeah, Dad, maybe you should," said Benjamin. "I mean, it's a good story and it makes it scary, but if he knows where they live, they'll have to leave the Emerald Coast."

"Yeah, and those lousy pirates even ate their goose. And Tip and Tap were so hungry, and, hey, how did you know about the goose, Benjamin? Dad never said anything about a goose. Did you, Dad? Did I miss something?"

"Boys, I'm sure your father knows what he's doing. He'll find a way for Tip and Tap to get out of this mess." Turning to her husband, she added, "Won't you, dear?"

"I don't know," said Mr. Kaye. "But Tip and Tap have been pretty resourceful so far. Maybe they'll figure a way out. We'll have to wait and see." Then he added, "Time for bed, boys."

"Great," said Benjamin. "We'll have to wait 'til tomorrow to find out anything I suppose."

"That's right," Mr. Kaye responded as both boys groaned. "But maybe you'd like to go to bed early tomorrow so you can hear the story sooner."

"Not tomorrow, Dad. We've got to stay up late. I want our last day to last as long as possible."

"Me too," said Martin. "I want to get up early and have all day at the beach."

"Yeah," agreed Benjamin. "Let's spend our last day on the beach. Let's not go anywhere."

"That works for me, boys. How about you, Mrs. Kaye? Are you up for the beach all day?"

"Absolutely. We can have a beach picnic for lunch and dinner."

"It's a plan then," pronounced Mr. Kaye. "Tomorrow, we hit the beach for the whole day."

"Yes!" cried the boys in unison.

"All right, boys. Time to settle down," said Mrs. Kaye.

Their parents tucked the boys in for the night. The light was turned out and, as they were closing the door, they heard Martin ask his brother, "Can we get back to the goose thing?" There was just enough time before the door shut to hear Benjamin's groan.

Mr. and Mrs. Kaye sat out on the balcony and, as they did every night, enjoyed the sounds of the waves crashing below them.

"One more day before we leave. It will be an adjustment getting back to our usual routines at home." said Mrs. Kaye.

"I suppose so," said Mr. Kaye. "But we have a nice life at home, too."

"Oh, I know. I'm just having a hard time letting go of paradise. I'll be fine when we get home. I wish we didn't have such a long drive, though," Mrs. Kaye added.

"It won't be too bad."

"I suppose you're right. But first, let's enjoy our last day at the beach. What do you say?" asked Mrs. Kaye.

"I say we'd better turn in now. I suspect the boys will have us up bright and early."

True to Mr. Kaye's forecast, Benjamin and Martin were up early and ready to go. By the time their parents were out of bed, the boys had assembled their beach essentials for the day. Their pile of supplies to take down to the beach included their masks and snorkels, the net for catching minnows and other sea creatures, and their pails and shovels.

"Looks like you two are ready for anything today," Mr. Kaye observed as he was pouring orange juice for everyone and setting the table. "Are you planning on digging more for your treasure?"

"We thought we'd give it one more try, right Benjamin?"

"Yeah, Martin thinks we should try digging in one more spot. I doubt we'll find anything, but it is kinda fun looking."

"That's the ticket. Enjoy the process, whatever the outcome."

"Right, Dad," said Benjamin. "Whatever that means."

While Mr. and Mrs. Kaye cleaned up after breakfast, the boys were given permission to head down to the beach. They wanted to start before it got too hot.

So the boys set out to dig one last time. But after a long while, they had to admit defeat. They weren't quite as disappointed this time, though. They had known it was a long shot and dug mostly for the fun of it. As they were about to quit and join their parents by the water, they realized they were surrounded by a group of boys who all looked to be a few years older than them.

One of the boys, the tallest and most muscular of the group seemed to be their leader.

"Well, well. What have we here? Looks like a couple'a punks digging for treasure."

The rest of the boys laughed. One of them responded.

"Yeah, Willy. Maybe they'll find some treasure for us. I could use a new set of diamonds and pearls, not to mention rubies and emeralds."

Everyone thought this was very funny. Everyone, that is, except for Benjamin and Martin.

"If we find anything, we sure wouldn't give it to you," said Martin.

"Oh, you wouldn't, wouldn't you?" asked the one called Willy. "If we wanted it, we would take it. Two little runts like you wouldn't have much to say about it."

Willy advanced on Martin. Benjamin stood between them.

"Look what we got here, boys. One runt trying to protect a runtier runt."

Again, the rest of the gang laughed. Willy continued to advance toward Benjamin and Martin. Benjamin was scared but he held his ground. Soon, Willy was face to face with him. He glanced over his shoulder to where the boys had been digging.

"Hey Jack, you know what the treasure hunters have found?"

"What?" responded the boy who had first spoken to Willy.

"They found a bunch of holes in the sand, that's what."

Apparently, the group had never heard anything so hilarious. Benjamin kept his cool and hoped the older boys would tire of making fun of them and go on their way. If only Martin would keep his mouth shut.

"Why don't you all go take a long walk off a short plank?"

Benjamin almost couldn't believe what he was hearing. But then, that was Martin. He would say anything to anybody, especially when he was mad. And the one thing that made him madder than anything was being laughed at.

Willy tried to step around Benjamin, but Benjamin moved with him. "What did you say, shorty?"

"You heard me. Why don't you just leave us alone and go on about your business, if you have any?"

"Right now, my business might just be to teach you some manners, boy."

"Yeah, Willy, teach him some manners," said Jack.

"Maybe I will," threatened Willy.

Benjamin was still hoping the boys would just go away. But the chances of that were slimmer since the group had challenged Willy to do something. *Maybe if I can at least even up the odds a little, we won't get totally massacred,* thought Benjamin.

"Hey Willy, do you need all these guys to help you with your battles?"

"I don't need any help," said Willy.

"You mean the rest of them aren't going to do anything if you and me get into it?" asked Benjamin.

"That's exactly what I mean," said Willy, not quite as fiercely. Benjamin's cool manner was making him have second thoughts. He had also been tricked into agreeing to fight alone.

Detecting Willy's hesitance, Benjamin decided to see if he could let him save face with his friends and still avoid a fight.

"Look, Willy. I'm sorry about my brother's big mouth. He doesn't like to be laughed at. I know you could probably beat me up. You know it and your friends know it. I've said we're sorry. How about just leaving us alone?" Benjamin hoped saying "probably" would plant more doubt in Willy's mind.

"It's lucky for you I'm in a good mood. I guess I'll let you off with a warning. Just clear out of here and don't come back. If I find you here again, I'll kick butt first and ask questions later."

Benjamin was relieved as Willy turned to walk away, motioning to a disappointed gang to follow. But then, he heard Martin again.

"Ooh, big tough guy. You want a piece of me? Bring it on. I'm *not* in a good mood, and I wouldn't mind having a crack at you."

Benjamin looked back at Martin, incredulous his little brother had taunted the stupid bully while he was leaving. He had given Willy no choice but to defend his honor against a loud mouth little kid.

"You should have kept your mouth shut when you had the chance. Now I'm going to shut it for you," said Willy.

Quickly and quietly, Benjamin gave his brother directions. "Stay out of this, Martin. Let me see if I can handle him. When we get into it and everyone is watching us, you run as fast as you can to get Dad."

"Okay," whispered Martin. Then added, "be careful."

"Who wants it first?" said Willy as he walked slowly toward them.

"Leave my brother out of this. You're the leader of your group. I'm the leader of mine. We can settle this between ourselves," answered Benjamin.

"I'll decide that, after I kick your butt," he said.

As soon as Willy was close enough, he took a mighty swing at Benjamin's head. Benjamin ducked down and, without really thinking, threw himself, head first, into Willy's gut. The head butt knocked the wind out of Willy. He lay on the sand, gasping for breath, unable to defend himself. Benjamin waited, thinking it would be unfair to hit him again in his condition. But, as soon as Willy was able to squeak out a few words, he motioned to Jack and said, "get'em."

But as the group of boys was about to descend on them, Benjamin and Martin heard a very welcome voice.

"Here, now. What's all this about?"

They had been on the beach, reading their books when Mrs. Kaye wondered aloud to Mr. Kaye about how the boys were doing.

"Why don't we go and see?" he had responded.

So Mr. and Mrs. Kaye arrived in the nick of time.

The boys stopped their menacing advance on Benjamin and Martin when they heard Mr. Kaye's voice. Mrs. Kaye noticed the boy on the ground, holding his stomach and breathing heavily, enjoying the feel of air in his lungs again. She went over to him.

"Are you all right, son?" she asked. "What happened?"

"Nothing happened. I'm okay. Come on guys, let's go."

The group of boys retreated, leaving the Kaye family alone. The boys gratefully thanked their parents for coming to check on them and explained what happened. Martin apologized for causing some of the trouble with his mouth.

"It does sound like you were using your head, Benjamin. I'm proud of you," said Mr. Kaye. "You were right to try to avoid the fight. Then, turning to Martin, he said, "It sounds like you let your anger get the best of you. Next time try using your head more than your mouth. Sometimes discretion is the better part of valor."

"Yes, sir," said Martin. And, as was often the case when he was speaking with his parents, he had to ask, "and what was that last part about desecration and valor?"

"Discretion," answered Mrs. Kaye. "It means sometimes keeping your mouth closed is the best thing to do."

"Ain't that the truth," said Benjamin.

"I'll work on it," said Martin. "And don't say ain't cause ain't ain't in the dictionary."

The rest of the day went as planned. The Kayes did it all – swimming, picnics for lunch and dinner, wave riding, snorkeling in the shallows, and catching and releasing minnows. The boys went to the pool several times for a change of pace, each time returning to enjoy the sand and waves again.

When it got dark, the boys came out of the water and sat with their parents on the beach. Mrs. Kaye suggested they each name a favorite part of the vacation. By the end of the discussion, just about everything had been remembered and discussed. They all agreed the vacation had been a grand success and couldn't remember when they had had so much fun.

"Even bedtime was fun. I didn't think that was possible," observed Martin.

"Yeah, Dad. Good job with the stories," said Benjamin. "They've been great. But I can't imagine how Tip and Tap are going to get out of their latest troubles."

"Shall we go in now and see?" asked Mr. Kaye.

"Before the story, let's do some packing so we'll be ready for an early start in the morning," suggested Mrs. Kaye.

No one really wanted to pack up, but there was no avoiding it. So, up they went to their condo, packed most of their things, and got ready for bed.

Out of the Frying Pan
and into the Fire

Captain Bowlegs was sitting with his feet up on the table, asking Tip and Tap about his diamonds. The boys were more scared than they had ever been in their whole lives. They had no idea how to get out of the fix they were in. Tip was relieved the pirates hadn't discovered the diamonds. Then again, if they had found them, maybe they would have been gone and he and Tap wouldn't be in so much trouble. A part of him wanted to just give the necklace back, but he still believed it might be the diamonds that could save their hides.

"I'm waiting lads. But I'll not wait much longer. Me patience is wearing thin."

The boys said nothing.

Bowlegs motioned to two of the pirates standing by him. "Mr. Rank, Mr. Fyle, please bring the boys closer to me."

"Aye, sir," said Mr. Fyle.

Tip and Tap wanted to back away from the advancing men but would have bumped into the giant smelly pirate standing between them and the door. The pirates grabbed them roughly by their arms and hauled them over to stand before the captain.

"Boys, you've been playin at bein pirates, scourges of the Emerald Coast, I dare say. And I must admit you've done a fair job of it. Tougher blokes than you have not done as well against me and me crew. I even have some admiration for what you've been able to accomplish, what with stealing from me, escaping me traps, and flying away like ya did. Aye, that was a sight to behold. But the game's over now, lads. It's comeuppance time, like it or not. If yer goin to play at pirate games, then you'll have to accept pirate terms. And the terms are these. Tell me where me diamonds is, or you'll be swinging by yer necks by that big old tree in yer yard. Mr. Smelling, the rope please."

Smelly John stepped forward and dropped a heavy rope on the table with a thud. One end was tied in a menacing looking loop.

"Sorry we only have one rope, boys. If we had two, ya could swing together. I guess you'll have to take turns."

Tip found his voice. "My brother had nothin to do with all this, Captain Bowlegs. I'm the one you want. Leave him out of it."

"Ah, the boy speaks. And he has the audacity to tell me what I can do. Well, young sir, beggin yer pardon, but I don't remember askin yer permission," said Billy.

"I just mean it's me you should punish, not him," said Tip.

"Oh, I know it's you what deserves the punishment. And I have a notion it's you what knows where me diamonds are. So, I guess I'll make my point first with yer lit'le brother here. That way, if seein him swing by his neck causes a change'a heart, you can still tell me where the necklace is."

Tap looked frightened, but said nothing. He knew his brother would not let him hang just to keep the diamonds. *Tip must have a plan*, he thought. *I hope it's a good one.*

Tip didn't have much of a plan. He did think they would

have a better chance of escape once they were outside. There was no hope of getting away as long as they were in their cabin with a whole crew of pirates, the biggest ones blocking the only door.

"All right, men, to the tree," ordered Billy. "And don't let go of those boys."

Tip was held by Mr. Rank on one arm and Mr. Farsythe on the other. Ears McGinty and Mr. Fyle held Tap. It was nighttime, but a full moon illuminated the clearing around their home. The boys were taken to the big tree that stood alone in the yard. Smelly John threw the rope over a limb that was about twenty feet off the ground. The noose end of the rope flew gracefully over the branch and came to rest just over the boys' heads. Tip struggled to get away from his captors. He kicked Mr. Farsythe in the shins and stomped on Mr. Rank's foot. But no matter what he did, the two pirates held their grips and did not let go. They did shake him rather vigorously to discourage his struggling.

"Last chance," said Bowlegs. "Last chance to save yer brother."

"Alright, I'll tell you. But you have to promise to let us go if I do."

"Why certainly, lad. I'm a man of me word. If I tell ya I'll let ya be, I'll let ya be."

"Well then, tell us," said Tip.

"How's that?" asked Captain Bowlegs.

"Then tell us," repeated Tip.

"Tell ya what?" asked Billy.

"Tell us you'll let us go, if I tell you where the diamonds are."

"I just did," countered Billy.

"No you didn't," said Tip.

"Yes I did. Mr. Smelling, didn't I just tell'em?"

"Aye, sir. They've been told."

Tap got into it, too. "No you didn't. You just said if you

made a promise to us, that you were a man of your word. But you never made the promise."

"I most certainly did," said Bowlegs. "And that's that."

"If you think you told us, and you meant it, you shouldn't mind telling us again," reasoned Tip.

"Why should I have to tell ya again after I just got through telling ya that I told ya?" asked Billy getting exasperated.

"Cause I think you're trying to trick us into thinking we've been told something, when really all we've been told is you would keep your word *if* you told us," argued Tap.

"And I think yer just trying to stall." said Billy. "Now out with it. Where are they?"

"I just don't feel good about the agreement we have," said Tip. "I'd feel much better if you would promise to let us go if I give you back the diamonds."

"You'll not feel much better once I stretch yer miserable, arguing, insubordinate lit'le neck, now will ya?" yelled Billy.

"Are you gonna let us go if I tell you?" asked Tip, clearly stalling.

"We've already been over that," said Billy, "and I'll not dip that crumpet in me tea one more time. Let it go."

"Well then, Captain Bowlegs, I can only assume I have your solemn vow that when I tell you where the diamonds are, you'll let us go and never bother us again," announced Tip.

"It would be my pleasure to never bother ya again, as long as ya promise never to bother me again. You two have been nothin but a pain in me neck."

"There you go again," said Tap.

"Where do I go again?" asked Billy.

"Wantin us to think you're promising, when all you're really doing is saying it would be a pleasure to promise," said Tap.

"I think I'll promise to hang ya and put us all out of our misery," threatened Billy.

"It's just not fair, is all," said Tap. "A promise oughta be a promise."

"That's it. Hang the brat so's he'll shut up," ordered Billy.

Smelly John grabbed the noose and pulled it down toward Tap. Just before he was going to slip it over his neck, Tip spoke up.

"I'll tell you. I'll tell you. Just don't put the rope over his neck. I'll tell you."

"Well then, where is it."

"Your standing on it," said Tip.

"How's that?" asked Billy.

"I buried it, along with the chest we found that was full of rocks the night we put the jaguar on those two," said Tip, gesturing toward Ears McGinty and Smelly John.

"You buried it where, exactly?" asked Captain Bowlegs.

"Just about where you're standing," said Tip. "Ten paces from the base of that tree, toward that big white rock over there," he added, pointing past Billy to a rock on the edge of the clearing.

"Hey, that's like our rock," said Martin.

"I guess it is," said Mr. Kaye.

"Was Tip making that up, Dad, or did he really bury the chest with the diamonds in it?"

"He did, Benjamin. He figured it would be the best way to keep his mother from finding it before he was ready to give it to her. Also, it seemed like a pirate kind of a thing to do, and he and Tap liked the idea of playing pirates."

"That makes sense," said Martin.

"Let's get back to the story now," said Benjamin.

So Billy ordered Mr. Farsythe to get two shovels they had seen when they were ransacking the cabin. When he returned with them, he and Mr. Gruntee began to dig. It wasn't long before one of the shovels struck something solid. In a few more seconds, it was clear they had uncovered the small chest Tip had described.

"All right, men," said Billy. "It looks like we've found what we came for. Now, let's see how well that rope fits around these scrawny necks."

"But you promised to..." started Tip.

"Did ya really think you'd be getting any mercy from me? If so, yer more foolish than ya look. String'em up, men."

Mr. Smelling grabbed for the noose. Prospects looked grim for the boys at that moment. They were both sorry they had ever heard the name Billy Bowlegs. They figured their luck had run out and they were going to pay the ultimate price for their pirate adventures. The situation looked hopeless.

Mr. Kaye interrupted his story here. "Now, have you boys been keeping track of the days and nights in the story?" he asked.

"What do you mean, Dad?" asked Benjamin.

"Well, how long have they been away from home?"

"Um, well, they spent a night on the *TELL NO TALES*," said Martin.

"Right, then they spent the next night, or most of it, in the cave," remembered Benjamin. "So, I guess they've been gone for two whole days and most of two nights. Why, Dad?"

"What would happen if you boys were away from home for two nights and we didn't know where you were?"

"Mom would have the National Guard and the FBI out looking for us," said Benjamin.

"I sure would," said Mrs. Kaye. "And woe to anyone I found trying to harm my boys. I'd put a serious hurting upside their heads."

The boys and Mr. Kaye laughed at the thought of Mrs. Kaye putting a hurting on anyone. But they didn't doubt her, either.

"So what are you saying? Are we finally going to meet Tip and Tap's parents?"

"We aren't, but Billy is about to."

"Alright! Let's hear it," said Martin. "This should be good."

"Yeah, Dad, lay it on thick," added Benjamin.

As Smelly John grabbed for the noose, he had a twinge of guilt. He didn't think it was right for them to hurt the boys, even if they had been a thorn in his side ever since he had come to the Emerald Coast. He was going to question Billy when, into the clearing ran a man and a woman, looking angry and very determined. It was Mr. and Mrs. Pettigrew. They were shocked to see their boys near the end of a hanging rope, surrounded by pirates. And they were prepared to do whatever it took to save them.

Mrs. Pettigrew called to her boys. When she did, Billy turned and saw them approaching.

With a dismissive gesture, as if nothing was going to interfere with his plans, he said, "Continue, Mr. Smelling. Little Pete, Big Pete, please subdue that hysterical woman and grab the man with her. They'll not be standin in the way'a me plans."

Still Smelly John hesitated. He especially hated to harm the boys in front of their parents. The men headed toward the onrushing couple to carry out Billy's orders. But the couple continued to advance toward their children, not to be deterred. When they met, the skirmish lasted all of about ten seconds and the two pirates were laid out on the ground, each one groaning and holding his head.

Billy saw these two were more to reckon with than an

hysterical couple trying to save their children. He calmly drew his gun and pointed it directly at them. "That'll be plenty'a that, now."

The Pettigrews stopped in their tracks.

Captain Bowlegs continued. "Am I correct in assumin you are the parents'a these brats?"

Mr. Pettigrew answered. "Those are our sons, and you will release them at once."

"I'll do whatever I've a mind to do, thank you very much. And by the way, ya have my sympathy for havin to raise two hooligans such as these."

"Call them what you like, and there are days when I might not disagree with your assessment," responded Mrs. Pettigrew, "but touch a hair on their heads and you'll regret it, more than those big louts you sent after us."

The louts were just now getting up, their heads still spinning. The rest of the pirates were surrounding the couple now. All except for the ones holding the boys.

"If you'll excuse me, Madam, I've work to continue. Mr. Smelling, ya have yer orders. Why aren't ya carrying them out?"

"Well, Cap'n, sir, it just don't seem right is what it is, sir. Hangin such young boys. Maybe if they said they was sorry, and ya got yer jewels back, we could just get outta here and be done with it. Maybe their parents will promise not to let them bother us anymore. Not to mention that ya did promise, sir."

"And maybe for good measure we could make them write on their slates a hundred times, 'I will not steal treasure from pirates,'" said Billy. "Are ya daft, man? After what these blokes have put us through, I'll see them hangin from the end of a rope or know the reason why."

"But Cap'n, they're children. And their mother'd be standin right here. I can't hang'em, not in front of their mother, I can't. Me own mother would turn in her grave," pleaded Smelly John.

"Maybe you'd like to join her, Mr. Smelling. I gave ya an order. Carry it out or feel the edge of me blade fer yer troubles."

"I can't, sir, do what you will. I can't have these boys' heads on me conscience," admitted Smelly John.

"Since when do pirates have consciences?" asked Billy. While he was arguing with Smelly John, Mr. and Mrs. Pettigrew saw their chance. With incredibly fast reflexes, Mr. Pettigrew broke into a full sprint, going right past Captain Bowlegs toward his children. Billy turned to shoot, and as he did, Mr. Pettigrew dove head first into a flying somersault, barely dodging the bullet that ended up hitting Mr. Gruntee in the left big toe. If the pirates thought his snoring was loud, it couldn't begin to compare to the howling that erupted from his throat upon being shot. Billy had a second gun pulled from his belt and was about to fire again when he felt an awful stinging on his backside.

"Eeooww!" screamed Billy, grabbing his aching behind.

Mrs. Pettigrew had taken advantage of her husband's diversionary tactics. She disarmed Little Pete of his sword. Then, she covered the distance between Billy and her in a few quick strides and, swinging the sword like a baseball bat, smacked Billy's bottom with the side of the weapon. When Billy reached down to rub his stinging bottom, his second gun went off, hitting Mr. Gruntee in the big toe of his other foot. Mr. Gruntee never did have much luck, or good luck anyway. He howled some more, even louder if that was possible.

Mrs. Pettigrew held the sword up to Billy's chest. Mr. Pettigrew had grabbed poor Mr. Gruntee's sword and was shielding his sons behind his back. They, too, were now armed, and Billy looked around to see several of his men looking sheepish and ashamed they had lost their weapons so quickly.

Captain Bowlegs was furious. His first mate had defied a direct order, he and his men were getting a beating from a man and a woman who should have been terrified of him, and even though the Pettigrews were outnumbered, they seemed to be gaining the advantage.

"How is this happening?" said Billy.

Slowly, the Pettigrew family moved as a group until they were shoulder-to-shoulder, creating a small square with their swords held ready for anyone who cared to challenge them. Mrs. Pettigrew held her sword against Captain Bowlegs' chest.

Regaining his wits, Billy slowly backed away from the tip of the sword. Mrs. Pettigrew did not advance. When he had gotten some distance away, he calmly gestured around him and said, "We still have ya bad outnumbered. If we fight, we will win and yer family will lose. I'll not be delayed anymore in takin what I come for. If ya try to stop me, all my men will attack ya at once. Right men?"

No one answered.

"I said, right men?"

Still none of his group answered. The truth was, scuttling ships belonging to other pirates or, at least, grown men who knew the risks of the high seas, was one thing. But attacking women and children, especially ones so stubborn about realizing when they were beat, was another.

Billy could see it in their faces. The men weren't with him. He was beaten for the first time in he didn't know how long. He hated to leave his diamonds when he was so close to reclaiming them, but he was given no choice. Dejectedly, he slowly walked away from the group, hanging his head and looking so forlorn, Tip and Tap almost felt sorry for him. The Pettigrew family held their ground, not knowing what to expect from the remaining group of pirates.

Smelly John spoke up. "I'm sorry fer yer troubles, folks. We should never'a been so bent on revenge we didn't realize we was after two young boys was all."

160

"Sir," spoke Mrs. Pettigrew, "I thank you for standing up to your Captain. I hope there's not too high a price to be paid for that. But my family and I will always be grateful to you."

"Thank'ee ma'am. And now if you'll excuse us, we better go look after the Captain. He might be needin our help with the ship."

"Certainly, sir," said Mrs. Pettigrew.

So Smelly John and the rest of the pirates left. Big Pete and Little Pete helped Mr. Gruntee walk as best he could. He gave Tip and Tap the worst scowl either had ever seen as he hobbled away. As they watched the pirates leave, the sun was just starting to come up on the new day.

"You boys have been busy the last few days," observed Mr. Pettigrew. "By the looks of things, you've managed to make enemies of every pirate on the Emerald Coast. I think you have some explaining to do."

Tip and Tap related all the events of the past few days, stopping to apologize on several occasions when their parents pointed out things they shouldn't have done.

"I can't believe you went to Mystery Ally," admonished their mother. "I can see we need to have a long talk about following our advice. You two might think you're clever enough to handle any dangerous situation that comes along, but you're not. I think that's been proven today. Still, it sounds like you handled yourselves well in a pinch. Though I'd rather you avoid getting into such pinches in the future."

"Don't worry, Ma," said Tap. "I've had all the adventures I need for a while. How 'bout you, Tip?"

"I'm just glad you happened along when you did. Where had you been?"

"Out looking for you, where do you think?" said their father. "We know you boys can get around okay and do a good job of taking care of yourselves. But when you didn't come home for the second night in a row, we were worried and went out looking for you. We saw the *Tell No Tales* down near the beach. It's going to take some work and a high tide to get that ship loose of the sandy bottom of the ocean. Anyway, when we saw Billy's ship, we suspected you might have something to do with it. And you might be in trouble."

"I'm glad you did," said Tip. "I couldn't see a way out of this one. Until you showed up, I thought we were goners."

"You guys were great," said Tap. "I've never seen you fight like that."

"And I've never seen my sons surrounded by pirates with a noose hanging over their heads, either. I guess my motherly protective instincts kicked in. But, it's not the first time I've had to handle myself. When your father and I settled here, we had plenty of skirmishes with unfriendly types who wanted to take our home and land away from us. We learned how to handle ourselves in a tight spot a long time before you two were ever born. I guess it all came back to me in a hurry when I needed it."

"I guess it did," said her husband. "Those scoundrels never knew what hit 'em."

"So, Tip, what is so valuable you buried it in our yard and Captain Bowlegs was so bent on retrieving?" asked Mrs. Pettigrew.

"I'd rather not say, if you don't mind. It's meant to be a surprise," said Tip.

"I'm not sure I need any more surprises. But I'll agree for now. Keep your secret."

"Thanks. Now if it's all the same to you and Pa, I'm awful hungry and I'll bet Tap is, too. Do you think we could have something to eat?"

"Now that you mention it, I'm famished myself," said Mr. Pettigrew.

"Me too," added Tap. Then he remembered Billy and the pirates had eaten all of their provisions.

"Not all," said Mrs. Pettigrew. "I have some secrets of my own."

☠

"I'll bet it's another goose," said Martin.

☠

In no time, the family was sitting down to a very passable meal out of provisions she had hidden away.

"Who were you hiding this stuff from?" asked Tap.

"Mostly you boys," she answered. "If I didn't, you'd eat us out of house and home."

After they finished their meal, they all went to their beds for some much needed and hard-earned sleep. None of them had gotten much sleep the past two nights and they all were worn out. Within minutes, everyone was asleep, everyone, that is, except Tip. He couldn't stop thinking about Billy Bowlegs. Tip had never appreciated his parents' love more than right at that moment and felt sorry for Captain Bowlegs that he had been orphaned so young. Eventually, he did drift off to an uneasy sleep, filled with dreams of lost treasure and lost loved ones.

When Tip awoke, everyone else was still sleeping. As he lay in his bed, an idea began to form. It was risky, but he knew he had to try it or regret it the rest of his life. He hoped he still had time.

Quietly, so as not to wake anyone, Tip found paper and a pen and wrote a quick note. He placed the note inside an oilskin pouch he sometimes carried to keep his valuables dry. Then, he left the cabin. He stopped in the yard on the way out before heading toward the ocean. He ran the whole way, hoping he would see the *Tell No Tales* still in shallow waters. When he got to the beach, he could see the ship had not yet been freed of the sandy bottom. Although the tide was rising, it would be some time before it was high enough to loosen the ship and allow it to sail away.

Wondering if he was being foolish, Tip waded into the water and began swimming toward the ship. With the tide coming in, the current worked against him. But he was a strong swimmer and, after a concerted effort, was able to reach the side of the ship.

Quietly, he pulled himself out of the water and carefully climbed up the side until he could peer over the railing. There were a few hands on deck. Tip could see the one called Mr. Smelling standing talking to a few other men. And he could see Captain Bowlegs, standing off by himself, hands behind his back, looking out over the side of the ship and into the clear water below. Tip was able to come aboard without being detected. He kept himself hidden as he made for the overhead doors of the hold, the same hold where he and Tap had been held captive, just two days earlier. Once by the doors, he opened one just enough to slide through and drop onto a crate below, but not before propping the hatch open with a piece of thick rope he found on deck, letting it hang down enough to allow him to escape when his task was complete.

As he had before, he used the hidden door to climb into the secret passage leading to the Captain's cabin. He allowed his eyes to linger, for just a second, on the bountiful riches Billy kept close to his quarters. Somehow, the treasure didn't have the same power over him now. Tip was glad Billy was up on deck. He hoped his plan would work. He let himself into the Captain's cabin and made toward the bedside table. He was looking at the picture of Billy's mother as he reached into the pouch. Then, the cabin door opened and in walked Billy Bowlegs. A more surprised expression had never appeared on anyone's face as was registered on Billy's. And a more fearful look had never been on Tip's face.

"So, me diamonds weren't enough for ya, eh? Ya had to

come back and try fer more. I dare say yer audacity will be the end of ya this time, young master Tip." Billy drew his sword. "And ya might move away from me nightstand. Yer not fit to gaze at me mother's face."

Tip moved slowly away. He took a few deep breaths, forcing himself to be calm. "Captain Bowlegs, sir. I want no more trouble with you. I have not come for your treasure. I have come to right a wrong."

"You may not want trouble, but it's trouble you've found," said Billy.

Then Billy saw it. Tip pulled his hand from the pouch. In it, was the diamond necklace. He handed it to Captain Bowlegs.

"This belongs to you, I believe, Captain Bowlegs. I came back because it was wrong of me to have something that means so much to you."

"What do ya know of what it means to me? I just don't take to folks stealin from me."

"No, Captain, I know this necklace is not just another bauble to you."

Then Tip handed Billy the note he had written. It said, "Dear Captain Bowlegs, I think it is a terrible thing you lost your mother so soon after losing your father. I couldn't feel right about keeping the diamonds he had given her and you had treasured for all these years. So here they are back. Sincerely, Tip Pettigrew."

After reading the note, Billy sat down and was silent for a spell. He held the necklace in one hand and the note in the other. Tip waited, hoping Billy would soften his opinion of him a bit and let him live, since here he was, Bowlegs' prisoner again.

"Ya must'a been hidin in me secret passage when I was talkin to me dear mother's picture. Am I right, boy?"

"Yes sir."

"If you were goin to return me necklace, why didn't ya do it at yer house?" asked Billy.

"I can't say as I know," said Tip. "excepting that I think I got caught up in winning. And, because I knew how important it was to you, I figured the necklace was maybe the only thing keeping me alive."

"Remarkable boy," Billy said, almost to himself. Then he said, "I thank you fer returnin this to me. I didn't realize how much it meant until I lost it. Maybe it's time I started noticing other things, as well. Maybe take some time off. It has been a grind lately, especially since we came back to this coast."

"I think my pirating days are over, too," said Tip with a wry smile.

"You'd make a good one," said Billy. "If ever ya need a reference to prove yerself a scoundrel and a sneak, I'm sure Mr. Gruntee'd be happy to oblige."

"I think I best stay away from Mr. Gruntee. He didn't look too happy the last time I saw him," said Tip.

"I don't expect he's any too happy with me either, come to think of it. I did shoot the man, accident or no, twice."

"So, what are you gonna do with me?" asked Tip, still apprehensive about his immediate future.

"I could take you prisoner, I suppose. But if I tried to hold you, you'd call up some wild animal to attack me, or fly away with the wind, or simply vanish into thin air. What chance have I got against someone who can do all that?"

Grinning sheepishly, Tip said, "I did have some luck escaping a few of your traps."

"I expect it wasn't all luck," said Bowlegs. "Still, if ya can't do any of those things this time, I don't figure you'll need 'em. I aim to have Mr. Smelling give ya a ride back to shore. That is, if he'll still take orders from me."

"Thank you, Captain. I owe you a debt of gratitude."

"And I, you," said Billy, "and maybe more than that.

I want to give ya a few things." Billy went into the secret passage and rummaged around a few minutes. When he returned, he had several things in his hand.

"Please give this to yer remarkable mother. I wouldn't mind having her in me crew. She'd be the best fighter I had." Captain Bowlegs handed Tip a necklace made of large, beautifully colored cut emeralds. "My guess is ya would'a given her the diamond necklace, but maybe this'll suit her as well."

"It will, I'm sure," said Tip, stunned.

"And if ya would be so kind as to give this ring to your father. I believe it will look quite handsome on him." It was a large ruby, in a setting of carved gold, with images of the sea engraved into it.

"Thank you, Captain. I'm sure father will wear it proudly."

Billy continued. "Your brother, Tap is his name, is it not? He is as brave as you are, if without quite the good sense you have developed. I hope he'll like this." It was a pouch of gold and silver coins, what Tap would call "pirate treasure."

"I'm sure he will. Once again, thank you," said Tip.

"And you, Master Tip. What is it you would ask fer yerself, findin me in the generous mood I seem to be in."

"Allowing me to return your mother's necklace without it costing me my life is reward enough for me, Captain."

"Well spoken, young Tip. Each time I think I am beyond surprise, ya surprise me once again. But I must give ya somethin, and if you will not choose, then I'll choose for ya." With that, he handed the last gift to a speechless Tip.

"I don't plan to be needin that anymore. Maybe you can make good use of it. Let's find Mr. Smelling. By the time he returns from takin ya ashore, we should be ready to shove off this blasted coast."

Tip and Billy left the cabin and climbed the steps to the

main deck. The men on deck couldn't believe their eyes when they saw their captain casually walking and talking with one of the boys who had caused so much trouble.

"Mr. Smelling," said Billy, "would ya be so kind as to row this lad to shore? He is no longer me enemy and I hope not the enemy of any of me crew."

Smiling, Mr. Smelling said he would be glad to escort the lad back to shore.

"Thank you, Mr. Smelling. And thank you, boy. I wish ya luck and woe to anyone who ever decides to cross ya. Go easy on them if they do, eh?"

"Yes sir, Captain Bowlegs. I'll certainly try."

As they made their way toward shore, Smelly John could not believe the boy, who sat silently and stared back toward the ship, had somehow returned to the *Tell No Tales*, made amends with the Captain, and, most remarkable of all, was wearing the Captain's sword.

Toward Journey's End

Mr. and Mrs. Kaye woke early, with thoughts of the vacation in their minds. Although they knew it would come, it just didn't seem possible departure day had actually arrived. The vacation had been such a wonderful – well, a wonderful vacation, in every way. They had done everything they wanted to do. And now it was time to go back to jobs and the last few precious days of summer before the start of school. Home to friends, chores, and ball practices, and all the things that made the Kaye's day-to-day lives what they were. They had added a new chapter in the adventures of the Kaye family that would live forever in their memories, and, of course, in the tons of pictures Mrs. Kaye had made the boys pose for. Although they minded at the time, Mrs. Kaye knew the boys always enjoyed reliving the vacation as they looked at the photographs.

The Kayes were bringing home with them a renewed sense of adventure and fun. The bedtime stories had awakened their imaginations and provided them with wonderful memories. Memories of snuggling in bed with your Mom, Dad, and brother, listening to each night's story unfold, and going to sleep each night, wondering what kind of fix Tip and Tap were going to get themselves into next, and if they would be able to get out of it.

"I wonder if the kids are up yet," said Mr. Kaye

"I doubt it. We were up pretty late last night. I guess it's time we get them up and going for the day."

Mr. and Mrs. Kaye got up, put on their robes, and headed into the kitchen. Sitting at the table with great big grins on their faces sat Benjamin and Martin. And sitting on the table, and doubtless the cause of the grins, was an old, worn chest – a treasure chest. Their parents couldn't believe their eyes as the boys enjoyed the speechless moment. Finally, Mrs. Kaye found her voice.

"Is that what I think it is?" she asked.

Martin could hardly contain himself. "It's a treasure chest. We dug it up this morning. Look at the top, it says *TNT* just like the chest in the museum. It's Billy's chest all right. We were right about that spot. I knew we were. We just hadn't figured things out quite right. But Benjamin took care of that. He figured it out and woke me up early. We went out there, and in about twenty minutes we were looking at the top of the chest. Can you believe it? Isn't it cool?"

"No I can't and yes it is," said Mr. Kaye. "How did you figure out where to look, Benjamin?"

"Well, something had been nagging at me, but I couldn't figure out what it was. Then, it came to me."

"What came to you?" asked Mrs. Kaye.

"What Mr. Fact said when we were at the museum. Remember he was talking about how Billy came to the coast and they thought their chest must have been from his trip here?" asked Benjamin.

"Yes, I do," said Mr. Kaye, "but how did that help you know where to dig?"

"It was the next thing he said, actually," said Benjamin. "He said Billy sailed back to the Emerald Coast ten years later. So, Martin and I calculated our next dig based on

Nat growing for ten more years. We were never that far off to begin with, but planning for the extra ten years was just the fine tuning we needed."

"Incredible," said Mr. Kaye.

"Indeed," added Mrs. Kaye. "Have you looked inside?"

"Not yet. We tried to open it but the latch was stuck. We brought it up here to get a kitchen knife to pry it open," Martin explained.

"Well, let's open it," said Mr. Kaye. He got out a butter knife, placed it underneath the latch, and jimmied the metal piece slightly. He was careful not to damage the hardware on the chest. It didn't take much pressure before the latch popped loose.

"Benjamin, I think you should be the one to have the honors," said Mr. Kaye.

"Thanks, Dad." Benjamin lifted the latch and then opened the lid. Martin, Benjamin, Mr. Kaye, and Mrs. Kaye all leaned over to look inside. The chest was empty except for one piece of parchment. In a strong, neat hand, was written,

Careless with me treasure, you'll find me not,
for every chest buried full, bury two that's got
but a note for the finder, the no good sneak,
he deserves no more for taking his peek.

W. A. B.

"Oh my," said Mrs. Kaye.

"Whoa," said Benjamin.

"Isn't that just like the signature on Billy's cabin door?" asked Martin.

"I believe it is," said Mr. Kaye.

"Oh my," repeated Mrs. Kaye. "I believe this is going to delay our departure a bit."

"Why?" asked Benjamin.

"Because now we'll have to call Mr. Fact as soon as the museum opens and let him know what you've found," responded Mrs. Kaye. "Don't you think?"

"Most definitely," said Mr. Kaye. "I'm sure Artie will be very interested in this find."

"But he might not let us keep it," protested Martin.

"Yeah, what if he wants to keep it for the museum?" asked Benjamin.

"I expect he will, boys," said Mr. Kaye sympathetically. "You see, a find like this is an important artifact and belongs near the place it was discovered."

"What's an artifact?" asked Martin.

"A piece of the puzzle historians use to understand the past," explained Mrs. Kaye.

"Huh?" asked Martin.

"Well Martin, it's something that is found years and years after it was lost or buried. When it's discovered, it allows people who study the past to learn more about that time period," Mr. Kaye elaborated.

"I get it," said Martin. "But I still think it should be ours. We're the ones who did all the work finding it." After thinking a moment, he added, "Hey, maybe we'll get a reward or something."

"I hope we get something for our troubles," said Benjamin.

The boys did get something. When Mr. Kaye reached Mr. Fact on the phone at 9:01, just after the museum opened that morning, Mr. Fact was so excited, he rushed over to their condo, leaving his assistant in charge. By the time he arrived, the Kayes had packed all of their things into their van, everything but the chest and the untouched note. Mr. Fact had to hear the whole story of the treasure hunt twice, while he studied the chest and the note up close with a magnifying glass.

"Definitely as authentic as the one in the museum, from first glance anyway," said Mr. Fact. "You boys have made a great find. What are you planning to do with it?"

Benjamin spoke first. "We were going to keep it, but Mom and Dad explained to us that historic stuff belongs in a museum. I guess we'll give it to you. Don't you think, Martin?"

"Yeah, I guess so. We sure worked hard to find it, though."

"I'm sure you did," agreed Mr. Fact. "And it's a very generous donation you're making to us. It will be placed in a special display after our experts authenticate it. The display will say, 'Donated by Benjamin and Martin Kaye,' and will be seen by over five thousand visitors a year. In fact, I'm sure the newspaper will want to interview you boys about the find. When the article runs in the paper, we'll have more visitors than usual, I'm certain."

"Cool," said Martin.

"How long will our names be on the display?" Benjamin asked.

"For as long as the museum is open, I suppose," said Mr. Fact. "When you're all grown up, you'll be able to come back here and see the chest and the note you boys found, signed by Captain Billy Bowlegs himself."

"Let's do that, Benjamin. Let's come back when we're really old, like Mom and Dad."

"Good idea, Martin. Let's plan on it."

"What a nice plan, boys. I certainly hope you two old codgers will be up for an outing like that at your advanced age."

"Oh, I'll bet we will, Mom," said Martin. "You and Dad still do okay for as old as you are."

"Gee, thanks," said Mrs. Kaye.

Mr. Fact bundled up the chest protectively, leaving the note inside. He was afraid to touch the ancient parchment. He carried the chest to his car, careful not to jostle the note inside. The Kayes waved goodbye as he drove off, clearly excited by this new discovery. Then, they got in their van and, turning to wave goodbye to the condo and the beautiful beach, pulled onto the road to begin the long journey home. Somehow, they felt the timing was right and home was the next place they wanted to be. Although they were all a bit sad it was ending, the vacation had been a wonderful success and they would always cherish their memories.

After a long, but relatively uneventful day in the car, the Kayes found themselves, once again, in a roadside motel, tired from their long drive. They had made good time after their delayed start and were more than halfway home. They decided to get up especially early in the morning so their arrival home would still be in daylight. The boys wanted some time to play with friends in the neighborhood when they got home. Getting up early meant getting to bed almost right away after they checked in to the motel. And going to bed meant it was time for one last bedtime story.

"Is everyone ready for the end of the Tip and Tap story?" asked Mr. Kaye.

"Ready," said Martin, Benjamin, and Mrs. Kaye in unison.

"Then here goes," said Mr. Kaye.

A Sail Set for Home

When Smelly John returned to the ship and to the Captain waiting on deck for him, he could see things were different and always would be. He guessed he had known it from the moment he defied the Captain. He just wasn't sure how they were different. Not yet he wasn't.

"The boy has been returned to the shore, Cap'n, sir. I'm happy to be followin yer orders again and hope you'll be able to overlook me defiance earlier. I just knowed it weren't the right thing, is all, hangin those lads."

"Fret not, Mr. Smelling," said Billy. "I'll not hold it against a man what holds to his convictions. You were right and I was wrong. I see that now. It took a remarkable and brave young boy to show me."

"Thank you, Cap'n. Glad to have things back to normal. In the mornin, we'll be …"

"No Mr. Smelling, I thank you. And things will not be returnin to normal or anywhere near normal I suspect."

"How's that, Cap'n?"

"I've been set to thinkin by the events of the past few days, and I've decided to make some changes. I've some things to prepare. See to it the repairs are made and we are ready to sail with the tide. I'll be in me cabin."

"Yes, sir, Cap'n. The ship will be ready," said Mr. Smelling. He gave a smart salute but Captain Bowlegs was already walking away, uninterested in the respect to his rank Mr. Smelling was trying to show.

"Wonder what's got into him?" muttered Smelly John. He walked out to the edge of the deck to check on the men's progress in making their repairs. "You there, Mr. Fyle, put some muscle in yer efforts. That goes for all of you men. We sail with the tide."

When Tip got to shore, he decided to spend what was left of the night on the beach. It was quiet and peaceful, and he wanted to be sitting right there to watch the *Tell No Tales* sail away. He sat and thought about the past several days, marveling at the adventures he and his brother had with Captain Bowlegs.

At first light, Captain Bowlegs was on deck in full uniform, except for his sword. Smelly John stood with him, going over the particulars of the repairs. He informed the Captain all was ready for departure.

"Very good, Mr. Smelling. Please muster the men front and center. I've a few words to say before we shove off."

"Aye aye, sir."

Soon, they were assembled on deck in front of the Captain and Mr. Smelling.

"Men," began Billy, "you've been a good and loyal crew these past years and I thank ya for it. I know I've not always been easy on ya, (he seemed to look particularly at Mr. Gruntee when he said this), but ya stuck by me just the same. We've had our successes and we've had our setbacks of late, as I'm sure yer all aware. But the events of the past few days have convinced me that me time has come. I'll be retirin and handin over the ship to Mr. Smelling."

A shocked gasp ran through the gang of pirates.

"But, Cap'n…" began Smelly John.

"No, John, me mind's made and I'll not be dissuaded. The ship is yers to do with her what ya will. I trust the men will follow you as loyally as they did me. I just ask ya drop me off at my destination before settin yer own course."

"Yes, sir. Certainly Cap'n," said Smelly John, stunned by the news.

Billy continued. "We've amassed a fair fortune fer our troubles over the years. I figure yer each entitled to yer fair share of it, now that I'll be leavin. I've prepared a map for each of ya, directin the holder of the map to the location of buried treasure. Each treasure is more than enough to support ya in high fashion for the rest of yer lives if ya choose. I would ask only ya help recover each of yer treasures before splittin up. I myself will take what I have with me on the ship, which is a handsome fortune. I know it's the more fer me, but I'll be needin more perhaps. I aim to do some good with me ill-gotten gains. When I find someone in need, I plan to leave'm the better off for it. So I'll not be feelin poorly about takin more than me share. I hope there are no objections."

No one said a thing.

"Good. Then Captain Smelling, the ship is yers. I wonder if I might catch a ride with ya to those beautiful islands in the Caribbean we visited before coming here."

"Certainly, sir," responded Mr. Smelling. Then he gave his first orders as the new Captain of the ship. "Mr. McGinty, would ya be so kind as to take over First Mate duties?"

"Aye, sir, it would be an honor," said Ears McGinty.

"Then let's be on our way, Mr. McGinty."

"Aye, aye, sir. Prepare to sail, men. Mr. Drifter, take a heading south by southeast."

Tip had been thinking about how he would miss the old Captain when he dozed off. It was first light, and his mother was gently rousing him. Mr. Pettigrew and Tap were there, too. Tip, startled when he realized he had fallen asleep, looked out at the horizon where the *Tell No Tales* was in full sail heading away from the Emerald Coast.

As they watched the ship sail away, Tip related the last of his encounters with Captain Bowlegs. His parents and brother listened in bewilderment. They were amazed at the gifts Captain Bowlegs had bestowed upon them and even more amazed and grateful he had given Tip anything but a sound thrashing.

"Farewell, Captain Bowlegs," said Tip, holding his new sword in respectful salute. "Farewell to the crew of the *Tell No Tales*. And farewell to pirate adventures on the Emerald Coast."

"Goodbye, Billy," added Tap. "I think I'm going to miss you."

☠

"Goodbye, Tip and Tap," said Benjamin. "I know I'm going to miss you."

"Yeah, goodbye to Billy Bowlegs and Smelly John and Mr. Gruntee and all the rest. They've been a fun bunch of mates to have on vacation with us," said Martin. "I will miss them all."

"So will I, Martin," added Mrs. Kaye. "So will I. How about you, dear?" she asked Mr. Kaye.

"I shall miss them," he said. "And I'm glad you all enjoyed the stories. Now it's time for bed."

And with that, the Kaye family turned in and had the last sleep of their vacation. In the morning, they arose early, quickly packed the car and headed for home.

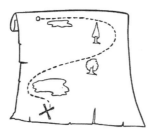

Epilogue

The Kayes arrived home safely, in the early evening on Sunday. After unpacking the car and their suitcases, the boys were released to find their friends in the neighborhood. Mrs. Kaye set about organizing the mail and newspapers a neighbor had brought in while they were gone. Mr. Kaye put all the beach paraphernalia away in the garage and the suitcases in the attic. When he had accomplished all his chores, he sat down to look at the week's worth of newspapers. Mrs. Kaye soon joined him and they sat together on the couch catching up on the local news.

When it got dark, Mr. Kaye went out to find the boys. They had been taking advantage of the last remnants of daylight to play whiffle ball with their friends. When it was too dark to see well enough to hit or catch the ball, the boys had sat down on the lawn and told their friends all about their vacation. Their friends were especially impressed by the results of the treasure hunt. Mr. Kaye called the boys in and they got ready for bed. Mr. and Mrs. Kaye tucked them in and turned off the light. As Mrs. Kaye was closing their door for the night, Martin spoke up.

"Hey, Mom and Dad, where are we going on our next vacation?"

☠ *The End* ☠

AND IF YOU LIKED THIS STORY . . .

On behalf of the Kaye family, I would like to invite you to join them on their next vacation adventure when they go camping in The Black Hills of South Dakota.

"Uh, Mr. Kropp?"

"Yeah, Martin, what's up?"

"Are you sure we want to invite everyone to come with us? Could get awfully crowded in our tent."

"There'll be plenty of room around the campfire to hear your Dad tells his stories."

"But what if they interrupt all the time like Martin does?"

"And like you sometimes do, Benjamin?"

"Well – yeah Dad – I do sometimes. But Martin interrupts way more than I do."

"Boys, don't you think we can be good hosts to our readers as they accompany us on our next adventure?"

"I guess I can, Mom."

"Thank you, Benjamin. And you, Martin?"

"Me too."

"So, would you like to hear how the next adventure begins?"

"I sure would, Mr. Kropp, Shoot."

"Funny you should say that, Martin. Okay then, here goes."

"Oh, and Mr. Kropp?"

"Martin, let him get started."

"Patience, Benjamin. What did you want, Martin."

"I just wanted to tell you to lay it on thick."

AND IF YOU TURN THE PAGE, GOOD READER, YOU WILL SEE HOW THE NEXT KAYE FAMILY ADVENTURE BEGINS

Hickok's Gold
By Joseph Kropp

Chapter 1
The Adventure Begins

Whatever "pitch" was, Martin didn't like it. He had heard people say, "It's pitch black..." And that was what he awoke to – pitch blackness. *It must be the middle of the night*, he thought. He reached for his watch, the one with the dial that lit up when you pressed the right button. He kept it on his bedside table. But when he reached for it, it wasn't there. Neither was the nightstand for that matter. Instead, his hand landed on hard, cold stone.

"What the heck is..." he started to say. The sound of his own voice stopped him. "Where am I?" he said, only to be treated to a fading chorus of, "am I's," floating back to him. He felt along the stone floor. From his position, he could just reach what seemed to be a wall. With one hand on the wall, he carefully got to his feet, using his other hand to feel above his head. Thankfully, he had room to stand.

"Must be in a cave," said Martin and his echo.

Now, nine year-olds tend to like caves, and Martin was no exception. The idea of exploring secret passages and tunnels appealed to him rather a lot. But, for the life of him, he couldn't figure out how he had gotten into the cave. And, if he were going caving, wouldn't he have thought to at least bring a flashlight? Just then, his foot touched a hard, cylindrical object on the cave floor. To his delight, he realized he now had a flashlight.

"I guess I'm not as unprepared as I thought," said Martin and the chorus, aloud.

Finding the switch, Martin observed his surroundings.

183

"Whoa Nelly!"

"elly – elly – elly," said the echo.

It was a cave. Martin was at the end of a narrow chamber that extended away from him, around a corner. And the walls and ceiling of this particular cave appeared to be made of solid gold.

"I'm rich – ich – ich –ich. "

Martin's mind was fast at work, spending his newfound fortune. By the time he heard it, he was past the new bike, the one with all the speeds, the skateboard, and the new soccer ball. He was working his way up to the sports car, mansion, and swimming pool, about to get to the private jet, when it came to him. Something, or someone, was walking toward him from the dark recesses of the cave. Something big. He quickly turned off the light. The thought of being in the pitch-black darkness with something else he couldn't see was almost too much for him. But he resisted turning on his light. He thought of running, but he was at a dead end. *Never really paid much attention to that saying*, he thought to himself. *I may be about to learn its true meaning.*

The steps were very close now, and they were bringing with them a flickering light. *Carrying a torch, by the looks of it*, he guessed. That reminded him of something. He had overheard his parents talking about a girl in his brother's class. His mother said something about carrying a torch for her. He wondered why Benjamin didn't just make the girl carry her own torch.

Parents were always saying confusing things, he thought to himself. *And eleven year old brothers are just weird sometimes*, he added. Those thoughts led to another. *I sure wish Dad was here. He'd know what to do.* Then, he heard it.

"Keep moving or I'll fill ya fulla lead," a strange, gruff voice ordered.

"I'm moving," a familiar voice answered, "but I'd be

obliged if you'd back the barrel of that gun up a bit. You don't have to poke it through my rib cage."

"We'll do what we see fit to do, mister. Ain't that right, partner?"

"Reckon it is. And I wouldn't be expecting no favors from us, neither. We don't take kindly to strangers sticking their noses in our business."

That's no stranger, thought Martin. *That's Dad!*

And it was. His father walked around the corner, followed by two mean-looking cowboys. One held a gun on his father. Torch flames illuminated Martin's end of the cave.

"Martin!" exclaimed Mr. Kaye. "What are you doing here?"

"I don't know. I just woke up here. I don't know how I got here."

"Likely story," said the man with the gun. "But no matter," he continued. "Getting rid'a two nosey intruders is no harder'n getting rid'a one."

"What does he mean, Dad?"

"I believe, Martin, that he means to do us in. These are desperate men. And from the yellow glow all around us, I guess they mean to keep their little gold mine here a secret. Wouldn't doubt the previous claim holder's trouble keeping a secret led to his demise. Probably at the hands of these two scoundrels."

"You can guess all you want, but it won't do ya no good. Now shut yer trap and get over there with yer little brat while I decide what to do with you," said the man with the gun.

Mr. Kaye joined Martin at the far end of the cave. The two men began to talk, ignoring their prisoners for the moment. Martin had never been more frightened in his life. It helped having his father there. But he didn't want anything to happen to him, either. He overheard the men talking.

"Why don't we shoot them both right now?"

"Naw, then we'll just have to drag their dead carcasses out'a here later. Too much trouble," answered the man who appeared to be the leader and who was still holding the gun.

"We could wing'em," replied the first man. "That way, they'd be easier to handle in case they got any notions about escapin."

"Now that's an idea. But don't shoot'em in the leg. We want'em to be able to walk. Aim for a shoulder. You take the brat. I'll take his dad."

With that, the two men leveled their six guns at Martin and his father. It looked like this was the end. Martin thought about never seeing his brother or mother again. They would wonder what happened. He hoped they wouldn't come looking for them and run into the same kind of trouble. Still, he wished he could see his mother so badly he could almost hear her voice and smell the sweet scent which always seemed to surround her. He loved that smell. It made him feel safe and loved. He wished hard that he could have those feelings one more time. But the two men were cocking their pistols and aiming right at him. He saw their fingers begin to squeeze the triggers.

Blaaam! He grabbed for his shoulder. But instead of feeling the wound and the pain he expected, he felt a hand, a soft, tender, loving hand, gently shaking him, and heard his mother's voice.

"Wake up, Martin. It's time to start our vacation."

HICKOK'S GOLD
AVAILABLE - SPRING, 2006